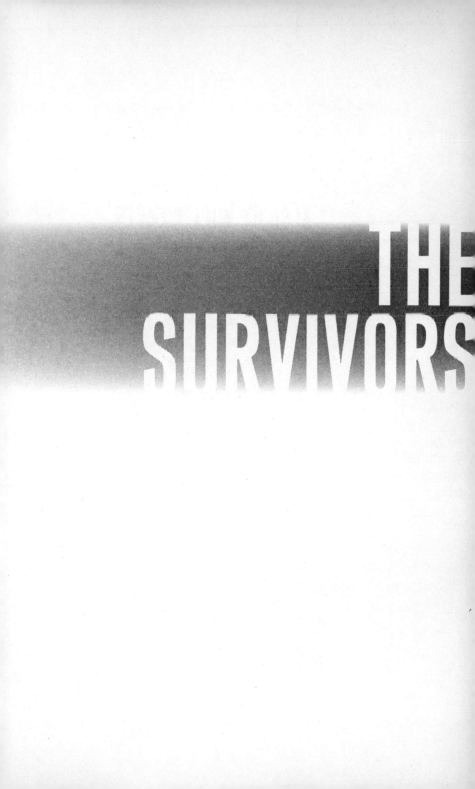

THE
SURVIVORS

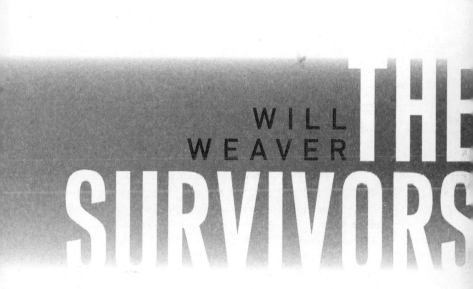

WILL WEAVER

THE SURVIVORS

HARPER

An Imprint of HarperCollins*Publishers*

HarperTeen is an imprint of HarperCollins Publishers.

The Survivors
Copyright © 2012 by Will Weaver
All rights reserved. Printed in the United States of America.
No part of this book may be used or reproduced in any manner
whatsoever without written permission except in the case of brief
quotations embodied in critical articles and reviews. For information
address HarperCollins Children's Books, a division of HarperCollins
Publishers, 10 East 53rd Street, New York, NY 10022.
www.epicreads.com

Library of Congress Cataloging-in-Publication Data
Weaver, Will.
The survivors / by Will Weaver. — 1st ed.
    p.   cm.
Sequel to: Memory boy
Summary: Sixteen-year-old Miles, thirteen-year-old Sarah, and their
parents find themselves changing in many ways as they struggle to
survive winter in a remote cabin, while keeping anyone in the nearby
town from learning they are living there illegally after the devastation
of volcanic eruptions drove them from their Minneapolis home.
    ISBN 978-0-06-009476-8 (trade bdg.)
    [1. Wilderness survival—Fiction.   2. Family life—Minnesota—
Fiction.   3. Minnesota—Fiction.]   I. Title.
PZ7.W3623Sur 2012   2011002087
[Fic]—dc22   CIP
                                                                 AC

Typography by Erin Fitzsimmons
11 12 13 14 15   CG/RRDH   10 9 8 7 6 5 4 3 2 1
❖
First Edition

Fun FAQs About Volcanoes for Kids Just Like You!

HOW DUMB DO YOU THINK WE ARE???

Q: Will the volcanoes ever stop erupting?

A: Yes! Very soon. Their ash plumes are 90 percent less than when they first erupted two years ago. ← *That's what they said LAST YEAR.*

Q: Why is our weather so weird?

A: From volcano dust and gases in the air. This makes some areas of the world hot and dry but other places cool and wet. One of our Founding Fathers, Benjamin Franklin, was among the first scientists to connect volcanoes to climate change. *he's dead. just like were gonna be.*

Q: If plants and crops don't grow, are we going to starve to death? *RAWR.*

A: Not unless you're a dinosaur! We just can't eat as much as we used to, which is a good thing anyway. Eating less makes us a healthier nation! *cheeseburger anyone?* *yes please, some with fries! yum.*

Q: Is this the end of the world?

A: NO WAY! And if anyone—even your parents—says things like that, what do you say back? "Stay put, stay calm, and let's get through this together!" *SUPER SIZE IT!*

Probably...hahahaha!

P.S. Remember to clean your plate at every meal— and if you have extra food, be sure to share it with your neighbor! It's the American way!)

YA RIGHT. (AND NO MOOCHING.)

Ray wuz here!

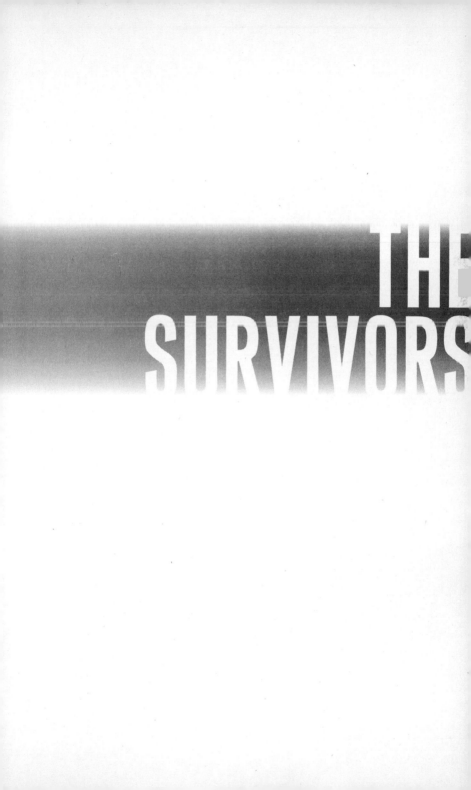

THE
SURVIVORS

CHAPTER ONE

SARAH

THE SKY IS NOT FALLING. At least not today. No yellow haze, no volcano dust—it's a hot, late-August afternoon with a mostly blue sky. Life feels almost normal, which means that Sarah and her brother, Miles, are arguing.

"—just saying, how many kids would go to school if they didn't have to?" Miles asks. He stops sawing to look at her.

"Lots," Sarah replies. She's watching him work, which always annoys him.

"Not me, that's for sure!" Miles says. He touches a finger to the bright handsaw blade. Tests its sharpness.

"You're still in school."

"Alternative school—which means I don't have to *go* there," Miles replies, turning to grab another board. "I can do my classwork at home. You should try it."

"And why would I want to stay *home*?" Sarah asks sarcastically as she glances at their cabin in the woods.

Miles doesn't answer. He gets all adult-like when he has a tool in his hand. Sarah kicks a pinecone, which skips across the ground in little explosions of fine gray ash—or tephra, as scientists call the stuff. "Maybe I like regular school," she says.

"You never did before," Miles says, bending again to his work. The shiny handsaw blade goes *RASS!*— *RASS!* back and forth against the wood. His tanned arms glisten with sweat, and the piney sawdust odor is strong but does not cover his stinky smell. "Back home"—*RASS!*—"hated"—*RASS!*—"skipped"— *RASS!*—"the time."

"Not all the time. And we weren't homeless then," Sarah says.

Miles quickly stops sawing. He points the shiny blade toward their cabin. "We are *not* homeless."

Her gaze follows his to the little shack tucked in among the pines. The trees behind are shaggy gray with the volcano dust that coats everything, and that has totally screwed up her life. Less than two months ago she lived in Wayzata, a western suburb of Minneapolis. Her family's big house in the cul-de-sac, her life of hanging out with her seventh-grade friends at school and at the Cinnabon in Southdale and the Mall of America and Valley Fair—all that now feels like a dream. Either a dream or else she is stuck inside a cheesy movie about a suburban family trying to survive an environmental disaster.

"Yeah. Some home," Sarah says. "It looks like it was built for trolls."

"Hey, think what it looked like when we first arrived," Miles says.

Sarah is silent.

"Trashed," Miles continues. "Now we've got gas lights, a front porch—Mr. Kurz would be proud."

"He's dead," she says sarcastically. Miles pauses to give her a glare but doesn't go off on her.

"Well, we're not dead," he says, "and thanks to him we at least have a safe place to stay."

Mr. Kurz—another character from the bad movie she's stuck in. He was an old guy whom Miles had met at a nursing home in Minneapolis during his ninth-grade oral-history project, or "interview a geezer," as Miles called it then. The old man had a crazy story about living in a cabin hidden in the north woods all his life; Miles was crazy enough to believe him; and their parents, Art and Natalie, were crazy enough to let Miles bring them all here. Then again, it wasn't as if they'd had much choice.

"It's great living in the woods by the river," Miles says. "Why would anyone want to leave?"

"Let's see," Sarah says. "A real school might actually have kids my age? Plus my cell phone won't work here. I can't call any of my friends back home."

"What friends?" Mile says. "And anyway, all those suburban fake-Goth losers you hung around with are going to be hunting rats or looking for roadkill to eat."

"Shut up, Miles!" she says quickly.

Miles does, which is his small way of apologizing.

"Plus a school has things like flush toilets," Sarah continues, "and hot water that comes out of faucets?"

"Our outhouse works fine," Miles says, not bothering to look up. "No pipes, no electricity—we're totally green. And what's wrong with cooking on a woodstove and washing in the river?"

"You tell me."

He stops to stare.

She pinches her nose. "I hate to say it, but you stink. Really bad."

Miles hoists his right arm and smells his pit. "I don't smell nothing."

"'Anything,'" she says. Since they arrived at the cabin, Miles's grammar and hygiene have slipped big-time. He hardly ever washes—never brushes his teeth. His hair has gotten longer, and now that he's getting older, his skinny chest is growing furry with dark hair. Every day he looks more like a wild animal.

Miles straightens up. "I stink? Really?" he says, now faking genuine concern; he sniffs first one armpit, then the other. He steps closer. "Are you sure?"

"Miles, no," Sarah says, edging away.

He fakes a growl and leaps forward to grab her. Sarah shrieks. He's so sweaty and slick from his carpentry work that she twists out of his grasp and races off toward the river. He waves his arms like a crazy man, and his hairy armpits chase her like two owls. Laughing, she runs down the path toward the river. Behind her, Emily, their goat, begins to *"Baaack!"* in alarm.

"Don't worry, Emily—I'll be back!" Sarah shouts over her shoulder. She makes a running jump into the water, hoping that Miles will leap in after her. It would be a service to the family.

But Miles skids to a stop at the riverbank. "Sorry," he says, "I got to keep working. Winter is coming, and anyway, you smell, too—like a goat."

"I do not!" she shouts.

"Goat Girl!" Miles teases.

She punches water toward him but it falls short, then swears at him for real.

"Sarah? Miles?" their mom calls from back on the front porch. "Everything all right?"

"You're in trouble now," Sarah says, emerging from the river.

"No I'm not." Miles quickly heads back to the yard.

As Sarah trudges, sopping wet, up the short trail and into the yard, her mother waits on the front porch, arms crossed. "Okay, what's going on?"

"Miles did it. He chased me," Sarah says, pointing to him.

Miles looks around innocently. "She's obsessing on toilets and showers again," he says, and shrugs.

"That's enough, Miles," Nat says. "I don't care who did what—just stop!" Their mother is small with blue eyes; and a red do-rag covers her curly dark-brown hair.

Art appears in the doorway and takes out one earbud.

"What's going on?" he asks. He's only a little taller than Nat, and has wispy curls turning gray over his ears; he shades his eyes against the hazy sunlight—he's an indoor kind of man, a musician, drummer for a jazz band, and a totally urban guy.

"Nothing," Sarah says.

"I'm so sick of these two bickering and fighting," Nat says to him.

"Listen to your mother," their father says.

"So what? Are you going to ground me?" Sarah asks her parents. "Take away my cell phone and credit card? No trips to the mall for a week?"

"Very funny," her mother says.

They are all silent for a moment.

"We just need . . . to pull together," her mother says. "Okay?"

"All right, all right!" Sarah says with annoyance. She isn't used to this new family teamwork motto. She used to have essentially no parents. Her dad was on the road all the time with his group, and her mother was busy with her literary clients—and it was just fine that way. Now they're like the *Little House on the Prairie* family—or more like *Little House in the Big Woods*: Everybody's home all the time. "Just tell me again why we're living here?" Sarah says.

Everyone knows it's a rhetorical question, but Miles isn't done pushing her buttons. "Where to start?" he says sarcastically. "Do you sorta remember when the volcanoes didn't stop erupting, how we had to wait longer and longer in line at gas stations? How fights would break out if somebody took more than five gallons? And how after about a year of volcanic dust in the air, the plants barely grew anymore, and all the grocery store shelves had big bare spots? All the 'temporarily out of stock' signs?"

"That the best you can do, Memory Boy?"

"Or how about the family down the road that was tied up and beaten by looters looking for food?" Miles continues.

"What family?" Sarah asks.

"Exactly," Miles answers. "I wasn't supposed to tell you—not that you were paying attention anyway— because it might have scared you. The looters did some really bad things to the mother and daughter, too."

"Shut up!" Sarah says.

"Stop! Right now!" Nat calls to both of them.

There's a long silence.

"Did you really have to do that?" his father asks Miles.

Miles doesn't answer, which makes Nat let out a long breath. "Oh, Miles," she begins.

"Forget about that," Miles says abruptly. "We're here now. And I thought—finally—we were all on the same page."

"And what page is that?" Sarah asks. She tries to sound sarcastic.

"We get out of the city and stay out until it's safe to go home," Miles answers. "Here at least we have enough to eat." There is no hesitation in his voice.

Sarah and her parents are silent.

"We voted, remember?!" Miles asks, trying to keep anger from his voice.

Sarah is silent.

"Okay. Then let's get with the program, people!" Miles says. He heads back to his work.

Sarah's father disappears back inside the cabin. Emily continues to hop and fidget, so Sarah goes over and gives her handful of grass. Emily nuzzles her long nose, wide-set eyes, and bumpy head through two slats in the wooden corral fence, and Sarah scratches her head.

"It's all right. Things are fine," she lies.

When Emily calms down, Sarah heads back to the river for a real swim; the river is the place she goes to get away from her family.

Among some trees on the riverbank, she takes her damp bathing suit from a tree limb and changes out of her wet clothes. Falls back into the cool, flowing water. Just when she's starting to relax, her mother appears and sits down on the bank like a lifeguard.

Sarah ignores her. Rolls over on her back and floats.

"I know this it tough," her mother begins.

Sarah says nothing.

"None of your friends are around. And we spend way more time together as a family than we used to," her mother adds. "We're all adjusting to that."

Sarah blurts, "Since when did Miles become the boss of our family?"

"He's not the boss," Nat says.

"Well he acts like it."

Nat is silent.

"Is it true—about that family?" Sarah asks.

"Yes. Miles just wants to keep us safe and get us through this—these *times*."

Sarah spits a fountain-like mouthful of river water. "'These *times*,'" she says sarcastically.

Her mother shrugs. "Every generation has something—some issue to deal with, like a war or a depression. Yours will be the volcanoes. Think of the great stories you'll have to tell your own kids—"

"I thought we were talking about Miles."

"Okay, yes. Miles gets pretty intense about things," Nat says. "Especially about our cabin because it belonged to Mr. Kurz—"

"I know all that stuff," Sarah interrupts.

"But what we didn't know was how much he and Miles bonded," her mother continues. "They spent a lot of time together. I think he became a grandfather Miles never had."

"Or maybe the father he never had?" Sarah asks.

"Don't be cruel," her mother says sharply.

Sarah doesn't reply.

"But in some ways you're right," her mother says. "We had our family issues. Maybe this time together is a gift. Try to look at it that way."

A small dragonfly lands on the bridge of Sarah's nose—she crosses her eyes and tries to focus on its cellophane wings, its bug eyes; but it's too close. The dragonfly's feet tickle her skin as it launches itself back up in the air; she itches her nose. "I hate it here!" she says. "I wish we were back at Birch Bay—our own cabin. That's where we're supposed to be living."

"Let's not talk about that," her mother says.

"We're going to have to someday," Sarah says.

Her mother does not reply.

"Okay, let's not," Sarah says. She takes in a big breath of air and lets herself sink to the bottom of the Mississippi River—which is less dramatic than it sounds. They are only twenty miles from the headwaters at Lake Itasca, and here the Mississippi is only waist deep. It's narrow enough to leap across in spots. A cold, clear stream with small rocks and tiny shells on the sandy bottom, and the deeper pools where the river bends. Underwater, she opens her eyes. Pretends she's a fish. Minnows with horizontal stripes and half-transparent bodies flicker by. A silvery shell the size of an ear glints like mother-of-pearl, and she grabs it. Underwater there's no sound except for her own heartbeat—and the muffled *"Baaack!"* of Emily. She sounds far away—where Sarah would like to be.

She stays down a long time, hoping that her mother will think she has drowned. It wouldn't be the worst way to go, sort of a cool, drifty death with all the dust washed away. She imagines shouting, splashing, hands reaching down to save her.

When she spews air and resurfaces, her mother is halfway back to the cabin. Clutching her shell, she emerges from the river, grabs a towel hung over the side of Miles's old raft, and dries off. She changes behind a little board screen that she made herself. On the way up the path, she yanks up a handful of thin grass, shakes off the dust, and carries it back to the corral. A nice treat for Emily.

Emily, with her soft, droopy ears, her Roman nose, her wide brown eyes and musky smell that Sarah has come to love. Emily was a "free parting gift" from the squatters occupying the Newell family's real lake cabin—where her family *should* be living right now. Birch Bay was their destination when they left Minneapolis: a cozy summer cabin near Brainerd that had belonged to her grandparents. The place they always went to on summer weekends. But this time when they got to Birch Bay, it was occupied by squatters. A family with kids and a biker and his wife. *You folks are gonna have to move on. It's a dog-eat-dog world nowadays,* the creepy biker, big Danny, said; and since he was a big guy with a big gun, and his wife was related to the local sheriff who would protect them, the Newell family had to move on. It was her family's most humiliating moment ever—especially for her father.

"But the bad people you came from don't make you a bad goat!" Sarah says.

"Baaack, baack!" replies Emily.

Sarah snuggles against her, but Emily is fidgety. Nervous. Her eyes keep turning toward the woods. Toward Miles, who is working across the clearing.

"What's wrong?" Sarah murmurs.

"Baaack, baaack!"

Sarah holds out more grass, which Emily munches on. But she keeps looking around.

"Lend a hand anytime!" Miles calls; he lifts another board onto his sawhorses.

"I'm feeding Emily."

Miles mutters something she can't hear.

"Look what I found in the river," she says. She holds up the shell. The inside curve looks like a pearl; by tilting it she can reflect weak sunlight.

"Clam," Miles says. "Actually a clam shell. The clam inside got ate by an otter or a mink."

"'Eaten,'" she says.

"That's what I said," Miles replies, and keeps sawing.

She gives Emily another handful of dusty grass—

and when she stands up, she sees a dog watching them from the edge of the woods. A dog the same color as the brush. All grays and browns and tans, like oak leaves. She squints to see him better, but suddenly he's not there.

It was definitely a dog. An old one, too. A gray muzzle and square head, which is how she noticed him—his large head with its up-slanted eyes. And a tattered part of a collar hanging down—she's sure about that. Somebody's lost dog.

She glances again at Miles, who remains intent on his boards. His shotgun leans nearby. She doesn't say anything about the old dog.

CHAPTER TWO

MILES

GETTING GOAT GIRL OFF TO school today will be a good thing. One less person to worry about. Plus she'll eat there. It's not as if they don't have enough food—he can always catch a fish in the river—but he keeps track of their supplies. Flour, cooking oil, salt, rice. Somebody in the family has to.

Just beyond the woodpile, a gray squirrel hops from to branch to branch, chattering, kicking up small puffs of smoke as it searches for pinecones. Far off, a woodpecker hammers: *tumma-tumma-tumma*. Close by, everything is quiet.

Too quiet.

Miles puts down a board and slowly straightens up. Chickadees nearby are frozen in place: none peck, none flutter, none peep. One of them has flattened its little gray-and–white-and-black body against a small tree trunk. Miles's eyeballs turn toward the woods, and his left hand reaches toward his shotgun that leans against the stack of boards; his fingers close around its cool, smooth, steel barrel.

His gaze stops on a bandit mask—not a real robber, but a bird sitting twenty feet away on a branch. Gray and white, with a black band across the eyes, it's about twice the size of a robin. *Songbird with hook-tipped bill and hawk-like behavior. Perches watchfully on treetops, wires. Impales prey on thorns and barbed wire.* Northern shrike. He has read about it in Mr. Kurz's bird book—it was checked on his list of birds observed: number 131 of 152 species.

The shrike fixes its beady black eyes upon a chickadee, one that has not flown away or hidden itself. The little bird is pecking at something on the ground.

Miles could change what is about to happen. He could shout, or toss a piece of wood to frighten off the shrike. But he doesn't intervene. This is nature. *Nature has its own rules. If you want to learn about the woods, you have to keep your eyes peeled and leave things alone.*

The shrike launches itself in a silent glide toward the ground, where it nails the little bird. There's a brief flurry of tiny chirping noises, but it's over in a second. The kill, that is. A moment later, the shrike lifts off carrying the limp little bundle of feathers. It's a bird-eat-bird world.

Before Miles returns the stubby .410 gauge shotgun to its leaning position, he quick-aims at a tree, then swings the gun 360 degrees around the clearing. Danny the squatter gave him the shotgun. Sometimes he thinks he should have swung the gun on Danny and shot him—or at least held it on him and driven the squatter families away at gunpoint. But he didn't. There were children watching, and he didn't really know guns then. But in truth he was chicken. Weak. His whole family was weak, and so they moved on—rode away from their own summer place. He spins and aims one more time at an imaginary bad guy in the woods, then sets the gun down within reach. One thing for sure: Nobody is going to drive them away from this place.

CHAPTER THREE

SARAH

FOR THE FIRST TIME IN her life, Sarah waits for a school bus. Back home in Wayzata, her mother drove her everywhere, as did all the mothers in the families she knew. Waiting to be picked up from the mall or the movie theater was annoying, but at least her mother drove a black BMW. Now, standing beside the dusty highway, she feels like a stupid hitchhiker. Like a homeless person.

Miles waits with her. Gun over his shoulder, dusty bandana around his neck, he bends down to inspect the fine layer of ash on the highway. To Sarah, the white dust looks like thin silk draped over everything. A weird kind of shrink-wrap. She wonders how the trees can breathe.

"Hasn't been a car along here in at least two hours," Miles says. He has yellow sawdust in the dark hair on his forearms.

"So?" Sarah replies.

"So maybe the bus won't come," Miles says. He glances toward the woods. "I should be out hunting, not standing around."

Sarah checks her watch. "It will come."

Miles pitches a stone across the ditch and into the trees. "You ever read that Jack London story about cabin fever?" he asks. "Two guys stuck in a little shack over the winter in Alaska?"

Just when she gives up on Miles, he always surprises her. "No, haven't read that one," Sarah says.

"Anyway, they get really crazy," he says, widening his eyes. "It's sort of like that movie *The Shining* but in a cabin just like ours!"

"Stop it!" Sarah's lower lip trembles out; she turns away so Miles won't see her cry.

"Sorry, Little Sis," Miles says, putting an arm briefly around her. "Just kidding. I promise I won't go crazy."

"It's not you. It's Mom and Dad that I worry about."

"Hey, we'll get through this. Next spring maybe we

can go home. Back to the suburbs." He makes a face.

"Do you think our house will be all right?" Sarah asks suddenly. "I mean, just sitting there empty?" Her voice turns weepy at the end.

Miles pauses. He looks off down the road. "If the scavengers don't find it," he says.

Just then comes an engine sound.

"Last chance to skip school!" Miles says. It's like he's glad not to talk about their real house back home.

"I'm going to school—I told you," she says, straightening up.

But it's not the school bus. It's a blue minivan, dusty, with tinted windows. As it slows, Miles steps forward so that Sarah is behind him.

"Travelers," Miles says, barely moving his lips. "Run into the woods if I say." In an easy motion, he shrugs the shotgun off his shoulder and drops the butt of its stock onto his boot; he holds the barrel loosely in his right hand.

The rider's side window powers down. "Hi there!" a woman says cheerfully; her gaze flickers to Miles's gun, then to Sarah.

Miles nods every so slightly.

The driver, a man, has tired, pinkish eyes and dark

beard stubble. Their children, two little girls, have their hair in cornrows with bright beads woven in.

"Are we there yet?" the smaller girl chirps to her mother.

"Shhh!" the mother says quickly.

"Mommy—that man has a gun!" the other little girl says suddenly.

"It's okay," Sarah says quickly. "He's a hunter—and my brother, too. He's just waiting with me for the school bus."

The little girls' white eyeballs peer just over the edge of the car window.

"You wouldn't know where we could get some gas?" the man asks.

Miles looks inside the dusty van; Sarah follows his gaze. The girls are squeezed in alongside clothes and luggage; the rear is jammed with stuff. "You could try Bemidji," Miles says.

"Not at a gas station," the man says, mustering a hopeful wink. "If you know what I mean."

His wife flashes a tired smile.

There's a moment of silence. Miles looks again at the little girls. "About five miles ahead there's a place called Old But Gold," he says. "Looks like a junkyard, but it's more than that. Ask for antifreeze. And mention my name: Miles."

"Praise Jesus!" the wife murmurs.

"No—praise you, brother," the man says.

The woman turns away, her tinted window closes, and the van accelerates very slowly down the road.

"Travelers for sure," Miles says, staring at the rear of the van.

"How do you know?" Sarah asks. "Travelers" are normal people trying to get somewhere safer. But normal travel—freedom of movement—is now against the law. People are supposed to remain in their own communities: the Stay Put, Stay Calm government posters are everywhere.

"They had Minnesota license plates, but the dealer decal said South Chicago Dodge. The plates were probably stolen."

"If you had kids, you'd steal plates, too," Sarah says.

Miles says nothing.

As they watch the van disappear into the dust, she leans against Miles for a second—and he actually puts an arm around her. He seems taller every day, and she's getting used to his smell—which is not a good sign.

"Be sure to feed Emily," she says, stepping away.

"I will. But I ain't milking her."

"She wouldn't let you anyway," Sarah says. "You have to know what you're doing."

"Whatever you say, Goat Girl," Miles says with a smirk.

"Don't let her get loose!"

"I'll watch her like a hawk."

"She needs fresh grass at noon, and make sure you fill her water pail."

"Okay, okay!" Miles says with annoyance.

"And I saw a dog," she blurts.

"Huh?" Miles said. He straightens up.

She hurriedly tells him about the old dog in the brush. "But don't shoot him, okay?"

"If he's a wild dog, he might be after Emily—or attack one of us," Miles says. "You should have told me right away."

"He has a collar—or what's left of one."

"When house pets get lost or dumped, they turn back into wild animals," Miles says. "That's how they survive."

"Like us," Sarah answers.

Miles is silent for a moment. "It's called adaptation," he says. "It's a Darwin thing. Or as Mr. Kurz would say, 'Root hog or die.'"

"Huh?" Sarah says, but at that moment another, louder engine sounds; down the highway the top of an orange school bus rises like a dandelion growing up from the dust.

"Remember," Miles said, "you're from—"

"I know, I know!" Sarah says. "Do I look all right?" she asks—as if her gun-toting, vagrant-looking brother knows anything about style. She is dressed in jeans, black tennis shoes (dusty already), and a white T-shirt. Miles stares at her for a long moment. "You look really, really, really . . . normal," he says, finally arriving at the word. He squints and looks closer. "I kinda miss your purple hair." He tugs her blond ponytail.

"Stop it!" Her punky-Goth hair has grown out over the summer; it's become full and soft from the river water, and streaked blond from being outside. She had thought about chopping it all off just before school but couldn't do it. She likes its weight on her shoulders, likes the feel of its soft rope on her neck. But more importantly, a ponytail is a key part of her disguise. She calls the look "Minnesota EveryGirl." It's designed to help her blend in at a new school. The goal is to be invisible.

The bus arrives in a cloud of fine brown dust. Sarah

covers her face and closes her eyes until the brakes hiss to a stop. The door squeaks and goes *ca-chunk!*

"I didn't know anybody lived on this mile," the bus driver calls out. She checks her clipboard. She is a sturdy, gray-haired woman not as old as she looks; she has man-sized hands that have seen some work.

"We live across the road and down a ways," Miles says vaguely, pointing in the wrong direction from where they really live.

"Name?" the driver asks, scanning her list.

"Sarah Newell," Sarah answers. Her mom has set everything up by phone. It's one of her skill sets; her mother makes a living, even now, as a literary agent. Once a week they go to town to the library, where she reads online submissions. The publishing industry is stronger than ever; since people aren't supposed to travel more than fifty miles from home, they read more plus watch way more television and movies.

"What grade you in?"

"Eighth," Sarah replies.

"Yup, here you are," the driver says. There's a gap between her front teeth; Sarah imagines that she can whistle like crazy. "Hop on—I don't have all day."

"Bye, kid. I'll meet you tonight," Miles says.

Sarah climbs aboard.

"Aren't you going to school?" the driver asks Miles.

"Been there, done that," Miles answers.

"You don't look that old," the driver says.

"He does alternative school," Sarah says, not sure why she feels the need to explain her brother. Other kids look out the bus windows. She is suddenly embarrassed by Miles's unwashed, shaggy hair and his stained, ragged Carhartts.

The driver gives Miles a twice-over look. "Regular school ain't that bad. Keeps you connected to the human race; know what I mean?"

Miles nods. "Maybe next year."

"Well, I'll take good care of your sister."

Sarah is hardly onto the top step when the door clanks shut behind her and the bus lurches forward. She grabs a shiny seat back to keep her balance and almost swings onto the lap of a bigger girl, who pushes her sharply away. "Gawd, watch where you're going!" She pops her gum with annoyance. She is wearing DKNY jeans and a Guess T-shirt and carries a gaudy Louis Vuitton bag, obviously fake. Sarah wonders if it's all for show or if she just refuses to get out of their time-warp bubble and acknowledge that the world has changed.

"Sorry," Sarah says, and flops into a chewed-up seat of her own about halfway back. She immediately looks through the window as if no one here is of interest, as if this is all very boring and she has ridden a school bus a thousand times. She swivels her neck around and sees Miles, the most paranoid person in the world, walking up the road in the wrong direction—the direction he told the bus driver they lived.

The bus is half full but very loud as kids call to each other across empty seats. Everybody knows everybody. Two gum-snapping girls in Calvin Klein T-shirts stare. "So, where you live?"

"Who, me?"

"Yeah, you," they say together.

"Back there," Sarah mumbles, jerking her chin over her shoulder toward the road behind.

"House or trailer?"

"Trailer," Sarah says.

"Double-wide or single?"

"Single."

The girls turn to each other and giggle wildly.

"What?" Sarah says.

"Sounds really cool." They giggle again and fall against each other.

You'd know, Sarah wants to say; but she turns away, pretends to see something out her window

"Trailer trash," one of them says.

Sarah watches them, reflected in the smudged glass, fluff their hair and check their lipstick.

Bemidji Middle School looks like a good-sized shopping mall. It's a big regional school, all the better for her to blend into. A giant American flag hangs limp on its pole. A "DARE" police car is parked so that everybody has to walk by it. Kids, laughing and bumping into each other, stream toward the front entrance. Parents drive away in cars, each with a small Blue Star decal on the windshield: The little blue star means permission to buy gasoline. Across the way, on one of the athletic fields, a tractor with a large, pull-behind vacuum cart hum along, turning gray grass green.

Inside the school the air is humid and close, as if the building has been closed all summer. There is no air-conditioning anywhere anymore; she hopes the classroom windows are open. Lockers clang, and kids jostle her as they stream by.

She heads to the main office, where there is supposed to be some sort of "new-student" packet waiting for her

"May I help you?" the secretary asks from behind a

small window. She has short, gray hair and unsmiling eyes.

"I'm Sarah Newell."

"And?"

"And this is my first day," Sarah says cheerfully. She glances around. There are more desks, and offices just behind them of the principal and vice principal.

"Where are you from again?" the secretary asks. She makes no move to look for Sarah's packet.

"From Park Rapids," Sarah says, faking a smile. "I'm here on the open enrollment option."

The secretary gives Sarah a long look, then turns to a box full of green folders.

"Hello, young lady," says a short, stocky woman as she passes behind the desks and comes to the window. She wears a loose purple dress and has a wide smile. "I'm Sally Wallner, vice principal."

Sarah nods and clumsily puts out a hand.

"Nice to have you here," she says. "Where in Park Rapids do you live? I grew up near there."

Sarah remembers not to swallow or blink. She has played a lot of card games with Miles, who taught her about keeping a poker face so as not to give away her hand.

"East of town," Sarah says. "Out by Dorset."

"Do you know the Handlemeyer family?" the secretary asks, still not smiling.

Sarah freezes. Remembers to keep her face blank. She has gone through the Park Rapids phone book with Miles and looked at the township plat map and the names of people—all to get her story straight—but does not remember that name. She needs a lifeline—Miles, who remembers everything (his family nickname is Memory Boy)—but she has to take a chance.

"No, I don't know them," she says.

"Neither do I," the secretary says. "I made them up."

The vice principal shrugs apologetically and smiles. "Janet's our office watchdog," she explains to Sarah.

"Just following the rules," Janet says, handing Sarah her packet. "Communities have to take care of their own. We can't be too careful these days."

"Actually, we can be," the vice principal says cheerfully. She keeps her smile on Sarah, though her comment is clearly for the secretary. "It's so important to remain optimistic and not let the dust get inside our heads. Don't you agree?" she asks Sarah.

"Sure," Sarah says. Anything to get this over with.

"Good," Ms. Wallner replies brightly. "Here's your

new-student packet. If you have any questions, don't be shy."

"Thanks!" Sarah says in her perkiest voice and then lets out a silent breath as she goes through the door and back into the crowds.

Inside the folder is her locker number, and she heads toward the eighth-grade hallway. Also among the materials is a round, green, smiley-face sticker that reads HI! I'M _____. She looks furtively around, then lets the sticker drop. It disappears under the trampling herd of sneakers.

"Hey!" a boy's voice from behind her calls out.

She resists the urge to look around, but the voice calls again.

"Hey, you—you dropped something."

She still doesn't turn, but then someone taps her shoulder. She turns to see an impossibly attractive boy: tall, skinny, spiky black hair, brown eyes, a dark I HATE ORGANIZED SPORTS T-shirt, and a wool plaid skirt—a kilt—like men wear in Scotland. It has some kind of large medallion as a buckle and a leather pouch hanging just below the waist. He's also carrying a large sketch pad in one hand; he bends down to pick up her new-kid sticker with the other hand.

"Me? I don't think so."

"Sure you did. I saw it fall," he says.

Sarah swallows.

Kilt Boy examines the green sticker, then glances at her packet.

"Um . . . oh. I think it's for new kids," Sarah says.

He smiles. His teeth are slightly crooked—but white and clean. A no-braces teenager. His stock goes up another hundred points. "No one wants to be a new kid in middle school." He wads the smiley-face sticker into a small ball and flicks it away without looking where it lands.

"Tell me about it," Sarah says. He feels weirdly trustworthy.

Kilt Boy puts out a hand. An old-fashioned, correct, business-style handshake. "Ray," he says.

"Sarah," she answers. "Nice, um—"

"Kilt," he finishes. "You like? My older brother and I saved up and went backpacking through northern Europe, and then up to Scotland where my dad's family came from. My last name is O'Keefe, by the way. Funny how my parents never wanted me to go anywhere until the volcanoes happened. Now it's like, 'See the world before it ends.'"

"Oh, Gawd," a voice says. "Ray's back. We were hoping you were, like, in juvie for the year. Or at least the alternative school."

"And miss out on another totally fabulous year with you, Mackenzie?" Ray says, imitating the girl's voice. "Never!"

Sarah turns to see a cluster of girls with look-alike book bags and a queen bee leading the group.

"This is Sarah," Rays says.

"We've never seen you before," the queen says, inspecting Sarah. She is a couple of inches shorter than Sarah and wears lots of makeup—way more eyeliner than she needs to. Her eyes are smallish and she knows it.

"I'm from Park Rapids. Transfer student," Sarah says, and begins to look through her stuff again.

"What grade are you in?"

"Eighth," Sarah answers.

"So, how old are you?" the leader asks.

"Thirteen."

"She's advanced for her age," Ray says. Then he coughs. "I meant smart—you know, advanced mentally?"

The other girls snicker.

"Shut up, Ray," Mackenzie says without looking his

way; she keeps her eyes on Sarah. "There are several new kids this year," she continues. "They say they're from around here, but I think some of them are Travelers. Are you?"

"What?!" Sarah exclaims, as if that is the biggest joke in the world.

"Does she look like a Traveler?" Ray asks.

Mackenzie gives Sarah a long look up and down. "No," she finally says.

"So that's settled," Ray says.

"Mackenzie Phelps," the girl says, thrusts out a hand.

"Sarah Newell."

"We have first-hour English; what do you have?" Mackenzie asks.

Sarah glances down at the class schedule in her hands and realizes she has crunched it. She smooths the page. "Biology." She tries not to sound too relieved.

"With Mr. Soames. That's in room 10-B," Mackenzie says.

Ray has not gone anywhere. He continues to stand close by, just watching. It doesn't seem to bother him that the girls ignore him.

Mackenzie looks Sarah up and down one more time. "You can sit with us during lunch."

Sarah smiles weakly. "Great, thanks," she answers.

"Or with me," Ray says to Sarah.

"Don't sit with him," Mackenzie says before Sarah can answer. "Ray is creepy. All he does is draw people—mostly girls."

"It's what artists do," Rays says easily.

"There are artists and then there are creeps," Mackenzie says.

"Uh, sounds like there's some history here. I should go," Sarah says. "Literally, I mean. Where's the bathroom?"

The other girls giggle.

Mackenzie points while continuing to glare at Ray.

Sarah escapes down the hall, and once inside the girls' room she chooses a toilet stall, closes the door, and locks it. She drops her jeans and sits down. Who knew a toilet seat could feel so good? Other girls come and go, laughing and flushing and running water. Sarah takes her time. When the bathroom is finally quiet, she emerges. In the mirror is a tanned Minnesota girl—so generic looking that for an instant Sarah doesn't recognize herself. She lets hot water run on her hands—silky, warm water—and all the soap she needs. Glancing around, she bends to the sink to wash her face. Handfuls of hot water steam her skin. "Mmmmmmm," she murmurs, then freezes.

Another girl has emerged from a stall. She is thin, with dark, short hair and quick-moving eyes. She looks at Sarah; her eyes go to the running hot water, the foamy soap. There's a long moment of recognition: *You're one of us.* Then the girl leaves in a rush, without washing her hands.

CHAPTER FOUR

MILES

AFTER BACKTRACKING FROM THE BUS stop, Miles pauses, then leaps from the asphalt to the road bank. He tries to leave no tracks in the ditch. Mr. Kurz would be proud. A slight breeze stirs the dust and softens the edges of his boot prints.

He angles through the woods, then to the hill above their cabin. Below there are no signs of life. His parents have gone back to bed—either they're fooling around or they're just lazy today. But white motion flashes behind the riverbank brush. It's his mother in the swimming hole, splashing, bathing. He turns away—not that he saw anything—and heads upstream along the ridgeline.

Carrying his gun loosely over his shoulder, he walks slowly, first planting the heel and then the rest of the foot: heel-toe, heel-toe. Goat Girl walks like an elephant: *clump, clump, clump.* He has tried to teach her the hunter's walk to spread out the impact, but she just doesn't get it. Or she gets it briefly, but soon it's back to *clump, clump, clump.*

The deer trail on the high bank follows the path of least brush, but with easy escape routes. Deer are not dumb. This would be a good spot for hunting deer, but the weather must be colder or else the meat would spoil. This morning he is on the hunt for a grouse.

Grouse are not dumb either. They do not like open spaces where an owl or a hawk can fly in and get them. *Look for grouse in the thickest brush, the kind a man can't walk through. A good hunter sometimes has to crawl.* Mr. Kurz's gravelly old voice comes into Miles's head, like it does several times a day.

He eases through the brush, its bristles sweeping his bare arms like a coarse broom. He pauses. Sniffs the air. A fruity, sweet-and-sour odor drifts up from the river's edge. He heads that way, eyes on the ground, until he realizes that the scent is above him: clusters of translucent red-orange berries. *Bears won't eat them; birds won't touch them unless there's nothing else to eat. So much acid in them that they barely even freeze when it's twenty below zero. But they make the best jelly and pancake syrup a man could ever want. You've got to know your wild berries if you want to live off the land. But why am I telling you this? You don't write anything down.*

I don't need to write things down.

You told me you had some report to write for your teacher.

I do, but I can remember every word you say.

So tell me what I said.

"'Bears won't eat them; birds won't touch them unless there's nothing else to eat. So much acid in them that they barely even freeze when it's twenty below zero. But they make the best jelly and pancake syrup a man could ever want—'"

Hehe. That's pretty good, kid.

I told you—I can remember every word.

You're a strange kid, that's for sure.

You're a pretty weird old man.

Hehe. Want to play cards?

You don't want to play cards with me.

Why not?

I can memorize cards, too. Every hand you play.

Hehe. We'll see about that. . . .

Miles reaches up and picks a single glowing-red high-bush cranberry—and pops it into his mouth. "Phaw!" He spits out the berry in an explosion of pulp and tiny seed. The berry is impossibly sour, but probably high in vitamin C. Miles marks this spot in his mind and moves on.

Not far from the cabin he sees tracks. He kneels to examine the round, good-sized paw prints in the dust. Dog. One of the paw prints is faint—almost invisible—and turns sideways when it lands. A bad leg. A limping dog. He follows its trail, which backtracks and meanders and then returns toward the cabin. Miles slips a shell into the chamber and stays on the tracks.

CHAPTER FIVE

SARAH

SARAH FLOATS THROUGH THE MORNING classes, then joins the rest of the students in watching the clock as lunchtime approaches. She tries to be casual with her glances. Someone's stomach growls loudly, and there is sudden laughter. The clock hands tick slowly on. Other stomachs begin to growl like a slow-gathering chorus of frogs. The one good thing about environmental collapse and reduced food supplies is that there are way fewer fat kids.

At 10:57 A.M. the first lunch bell rings. The students lurch up from their desks, and she joins the giant snake of bodies speed walking to the cafeteria. Last year she hardly ever ate the school's lunch; and when she did, she was never in any hurry. This year she walks fast and keeps others from cutting ahead of her. Lunch is serious now.

At the counter a woman wearing a hairnet and clear plastic gloves dishes out spoonfuls of a cheesy hot dish that has clumps of mystery meat. The next woman in line piles on soggy, limp green beans. After that it's the potato woman—whose face looks like a potato. But any food is a nice change from river fish and rice. The other students in line carefully watch the cafeteria women dish out their food.

"Hey, he got more potatoes than me!" someone says.

"Keep moving," the potato-scooper woman says.

With her tray, Sarah turns toward the crowded cafeteria tables. Always the big question: where to sit. She doesn't see Mackenzie's group. She drifts along, looking for an open space on the benches.

Ray O'Keefe is seated at a table with kids of many colors: a peroxide blond Latino boy; a skinny Gothy girl with long black hair with cherry-red streaks; a couple of black-haired Native American boys; two white girls in dreads and tie-dyed T-shirts; one fat girl between two scrawny, bushy-haired white boys. Ray has a sketch pad open and a pencil in his hand.

"Sarah—here we are!" calls Mackenzie. She is moving along with a tray, and uses it to herd Sarah away from Ray's table. Sarah glances over her shoulder helplessly at Ray.

He shrugs and turns back to his friends.

"You weren't actually going to sit by him, were you?" Mackenzie says, plopping down her tray.

Sarah stammers, "I—I just heard someone call my name, you know. . . ."

"Gawd, imagine having to sit through a whole lunch period with those freaks," says another in girl.

"Torture," another says.

"So what's your deal with Ray?" Sarah asks Mackenzie.

"Nothing," Mackenzie says.

"You're just mad because he's never asked you." One of the girls giggles.

"Asked what?" Sarah says.

"To pose."

"Pose?" Sarah asks.

"Like, model—so he can draw her."

"You mean a life model?"

"Huh?" one of the girls says.

"Nude," Sarah says.

The table full of girls shrieks with laughter; one of them coughs up food, which only brings more laughter.

"No, not nude!" Mackenzie says when the girls quiet down. "Though that's probably what he really wants."

"He's an amazing artist," one of the girls says softly. "I mean, it was fun letting him draw me."

"Me, too," another says. "He's gonna be famous someday."

Mackenzie turns to them with a long glare; they quickly look down at their food.

"So what did you do in Park Rapids?" Mackenzie says to Sarah. "Any sports?"

"Not really," Sarah says. "I was homeschooled, actually," she explains, and rolls her eyes.

"So why'd you come here?" Mackenzie asks.

"I told my parents I'd sue them if I had to stay at home another year," Sarah says.

The girls giggle.

"Well, since you're here, you clearly need to know stuff about this school," Mackenzie says. She looks around the cafeteria. "See that cute guy with the buzz cut over there? That's Django. Isn't that the coolest name ever? He's really good at basketball, and we, you know, go out once in a while."

"They're going steady!" one of the girls says, and everyone laughs.

"And next to him, that guy in the red T-shirt? He's Derek."

Sarah lets Mackenzie rattle on and concentrates on her lunch. She scarfs down everything. She was never part of the clean-plate club BV (Before Volcanoes), but now, even bad cafeteria food is too precious to be tossed. She puts her tray on the conveyor belt, where all the other plates and dishes are as empty as if a dog has licked them shiny.

Ray catches up with her in the hallway. "Nice lunch?"

"Sort of."

"So you're friends with Mackenzie now?"

"Maybe."

"I gotta say, they just don't seem like your crowd."

"What's my crowd?"

"I don't know yet," he says. His dark eyes probe hers; it's as if he can see all the way through her. He reaches out and puts a finger on the ancient, faded NOFX patch stitched onto her backpack—and also brushes her arm. Her bare skin tingles.

"So what's *your* crowd?" she replies quickly. Her arm

burns where his hand touched her, and she feels her face go hot, too.

"Probably not this whole school," he says quickly with a glance around them. "I'd really like to be at the arts school in Minneapolis; I have my application in."

She laughs.

"What?" he asks.

"Nothing," she says quickly. "I mean, you do seem sort of . . . artsy. A guy who wears kilts."

"It's my disguise," he says.

She's totally warm and blushing and very short on words.

"What's yours?" he asks.

"My disguise?"

He waits for her reply.

"What makes you think I have one?" she throws back.

"Everybody does," Ray says with his killer grin.

CHAPTER SIX

MILES

TUNK. TUNK-TUNK.

At the sounds, Miles drops low behind some brush. He is following the wild dog's tracks along the riverbank away from his mother, but now he pauses to listen. On the river, coming closer, *tunka-tunk*: the noise comes from canoe paddles.

Clumsy paddling. Miles looks over his shoulder, back toward the cabin and the riverbank where his mother might still be having her morning swim. He eases backward to take a shortcut home so that he can call out to warn her. On the river, the woman's voice says, "I think I had a bite!"

"Did it jerk back and forth?"

"No, just kind of a tug," she answers.

"Probably a weed. Check your hook." The guy makes a clumsy cast with his fishing pole.

They're a youngish couple who clearly haven't fished much. They seem harmless enough, but at a bend in the river, Miles leaves the deer trail and angles straight across to get ahead of the canoeists. When he comes to the edge of the clearing, his mother is fully dressed. But she is sitting on the riverbank with a towel draped around her hair, and with a small bottle and brush she is doing her toenails.

He waves with both hands, but she's engrossed in her toes.

By then it's too late: A canoe paddle goes *clonk!*, and his mother suddenly looks up as the canoe comes around the bend.

"Hello!" the woman says as the canoe approaches.

"Hi there," Nat says. She doesn't scramble or run, but glances around for Miles; she spots him but doesn't give him away. Miles shrinks farther back into the trees.

"What a surprise!" the young woman in the bow says. She has reddish hair, lots of it, tucked under a scarf, but her face is thin.

"Yes!" Nat says.

The man in the stern steers the canoe to the shore; its nose grinds into the sand. "I didn't think anyone lived way out here," he says, looking up the bank. He has a short, dark beard and hollow cheeks and is wearing a baseball cap. Miles follows his gaze; luckily there is no smoke rising from the cookstove. The only sign of human life is the faint, narrow path leading uphill from the river.

"Live out here?" Nat says. She manufactures a laugh. "I don't think so. My family and I are just camping for a couple of nights. You know, get away from it all."

"Same with us!" the woman says quickly. "We're just out fishing."

"Trying to," her partner adds. He keeps looking up the trail—trying to see what's behind the trees. "Must be a nice place to camp."

Miles steps out from the trees.

"My son," Nat says.

The woman reaches down to the bottom of the canoe; Miles tightens his grip on the shotgun, but she lifts up a bundle that emits a tiny, perfect wail.

"A baby—congratulations," Natalie says.

"Thanks," the woman says, holding her baby tightly as Miles approaches.

"Howdy," he says.

"Hey," the canoe couple say simultaneously to Miles.

"So how old is your baby?" Nat asks pleasantly.

"Four months," the mother says. The baby is totally wrapped in a blanket; its face is not visible.

"Believe it or not, this guy used to be that small," Nat says as Miles arrives at the river's edge. The fishing couple look warily at Miles's shotgun.

"Any luck?" Miles asks in the universal greeting to people in a boat with fishing poles.

"Nothing," the guy answers. He seems defeated—as if he's totally out of his element.

"The fish are in the weed beds, not in the open channel," Miles says. "For bass, use something silvery that looks like a minnow. Northern pike like to hang right on the weed lines. They'll hit a red-and-white spoon."

"Thanks!" the woman says.

"Well, we'd better keep fishing," the man says. "Have a nice day camping."

Miles and his mother watch the pair head downstream. The man paddles, and the woman bends closer around her baby. It cries once more with the same little wail; the mother glances over her shoulder as the canoe slides out of sight around a bend.

"Where did *they* come from?" Natalie says to Miles.

"Upriver. Clanging their paddles and talking loud all the way."

"Sorry," his mother says. "I had the towel over my ears."

Miles shrugs. "What if they'd been squatters?"

His mother shrugs and takes his arm. "I've got a scary-looking son in the woods with a gun," she says.

"I can't be around all the time."

"I know," she answers. "But they weren't squatters or bad guys, were they? Just a nice young family."

Miles glances behind. "The fewer people who know we're here, the better."

"You're starting to sound like Mr. Kurz," his mother teases.

"And look what happened to him," Miles mutters. "One trip to the big city for his sister's funeral and his family slaps him in an old folks' home."

"Hey—where are we going?" his mother says as Miles steers her off the trail.

"Let's not use the same path all the time. The more

we use it, the more obvious it becomes."

"Yes, Mr. Kurz," his mother says.

When the cabin is in sight, he pauses. "I'm gonna head back to the woods for a while."

"Be careful," his mother says automatically.

When she is out of sight, Miles hurries down a deer trail along the river. There was something slightly off about that little family of three. Something weird that he can't put his finger on.

It takes a few minutes before he catches a glimpse of the canoe through the riverbank brush, but in another minute he's ahead of it and crouched behind a fallen tree only a few yards from the water where they will pass.

"—be camping way out here?" the woman asks.

"They're not camping," the man says harshly. "I told you—they gotta be living there. They're probably Travelers. Or squatters."

"So?" the woman says.

"We should threaten to turn them in," the guy says. "I'll bet they've got food stashed for winter—and they'd give us some."

"That scary-looking kid had a gun," the woman says.

The man is silent.

"And anyway, we've got something better than a gun," the woman says. She reaches down. The baby cries again—the same perfect little wail.

Miles swallows a grunt of recognition: He remembers that sound. It's from a doll, a You & Me brand, fourteen-inch, battery-operated crying doll; Miles knows, because Sarah used to have one—and the stupid thing drove him nuts.

"Baby's got to eat," the woman says. "They love you at the grocery store, too, don't they?" she says, faking baby talk.

The guy ignores her. He swings the canoe sideways in order to look upstream. "I still say we should go back and case the place. Sneak up and see what they got."

"But who would watch the baby?" the woman asks; it's supposed to be a joke, but it's clear that she wants no part of this.

The man doesn't answer; he paddles backward so that the canoe holds steady in the current.

"Please, Jeremy," she says. "We're not, like, thieves."

He sets his jaw. "Yeah, well, the world is different now." With a couple of hard thrusts of his paddle, he turns the canoe toward shore and beaches it on the sand with a scraping sound.

"I'm not going with you!" the woman says.

"Fine!" the guy says. "Stay here."

"Jeremy—you don't know who they are or what's out there!" the woman says.

The man ignores her and puts one leg over the side of the canoe. Which is when Miles fires—a warning shot—into the river beside him. Water sprays the couple, and the woman sucks in a shriek as the man topples backward into the canoe. Miles steps into the open and trains the gun on them. His .410 holds only one shell, but he would have plenty of time to reload.

"She's right!" Miles says. "You just don't know who's out there."

"Please! Don't shoot us!" the woman whimpers.

Miles is silent.

The man's Adam's apple bobs up and down like a crazy yo-yo. He's lying on his back in the canoe like an upturned turtle.

"Show me some ID," Miles says.

"ID?" the man asks. His voice is thin and quaky.

"For God's sakes, give him your wallet," the woman breathes.

The man digs into a rear pocket, then tosses the wallet to Miles; keeping one eye on the canoeists, he crouches on the bank, fishes out the guy's driver's license, looks at it. Then he tosses back the wallet.

"Aren't you going to rob us?" the woman says weakly.

"Please—just shut up," the man whispers at her.

"No. Just want to see where you live," Miles says. "So I know where to come. You know, in case—"

"Hey, we were just blowing smoke!" the man says. "We won't turn you in or cause you any trouble."

"We'll forget we ever saw you!" the woman adds in a rush of words.

Miles pauses. "Promise?"

"Yes!" the couple say at the same time.

"Cross your heart and hope not to die?" He looks once more at the address on the license. "Jeremy Barchers?"

The two are white-faced now and can only nod up and down.

He pockets the driver's license—keeps it.

"Okay. Works for me," Miles says. Gun in hand, with his left boot he pushes their canoe sharply off the sand and into the current. "Have a nice day."

The couple's canoe paddles clang and bang rapidly as they head downstream.

"And take good care of your baby!" he calls after them.

When the canoe goes around the bend and out of sight, Miles lets out a long breath. His hands are shaky. He puts down the gun and sits on the riverbank. It takes a few minutes before he's ready to head home.

Back at the cabin, his father is out by the sawmill, actually working. He and Nat are sorting boards per Miles's instruction. They look up as Miles comes out of the woods. "I heard you shoot," his father says. "Did you get anything?"

Miles pauses. "No," he says with a glance toward his mother. "I missed."

CHAPTER SEVEN

SARAH

THE BUS RIDE HOME HAS less coughing because several kids have stayed for after-school activities. The ones who remain look shabby and geeky and would definitely not fit in with Mackenzie's crowd. Some of them look like farm kids; the boys wear sweat-stained seed caps as well as NASCAR, Caterpillar, and Ducks Unlimited T-shirts. She sits up front as far away from them as she can.

"No sports or after-school stuff for you, honey?" the woman driver says, startling Sarah.

"Nope." She has been staring out the window at the

minivans. At the Blue Star families. Families who don't hide out in the woods.

"Not the sports type?" the driver asks, stomping a pedal and shifting gears with a quick yank of her forearm.

"Not really. Plus I sorta have to help out at home," Sarah says. She thinks about Emily for the first time all day.

"Not enough kids do that nowadays. They think life is all about them, but I guess I was that way, too," the driver says.

Sarah is silent.

"My kids are grown now. Two grandbabies. I wish they lived closer, because we can't go see them now." She sneezes. "That's the worst part of this damn dust— the travel restrictions."

Sarah is silent.

"But they say the worst is over," the woman continues; she leans forward to look at the sky through her smudged windshield.

"I hope so," Sarah murmurs.

"I really miss seeing my grandkids," the driver continues. "Family is all any of us really have."

After forty-five minutes and several brake-squeaking stops, Sarah sits up suddenly; she must have dozed briefly—and she wonders if the bus driver will remember her stop. It's not as if they have a big driveway and mailbox.

"There's your brother," the driver says, squinting ahead.

Sarah is filled with a rush of relief—which quickly fades as she sees Miles standing shirtless with a canteen hanging off his shoulder. Gun over his shoulder, bandana across his nose because of the highway dust, and holding a tall, knobby walking stick, he looks like an extra from one of those old Mad Max movies.

"Regular school wouldn't hurt that boy," observes the driver as she brakes the bus.

"No kidding," Sarah says.

"But he watches out for you—that's a good thing nowadays," the driver says.

"Thanks for the ride," Sarah says, and steps down.

"Hey, Goat Girl, how was your first day at school?" Miles says, pulling down his bandana. His face is streaked with dust and sweat, and he's stinkier than ever.

"Okay," Sarah says with a shrug.

"There's still time for you, son," the driver calls down

to Miles through the open door. "You're only one day behind."

"No thanks," Miles says.

The driver laughs, then closes the door and drives on.

"Is Emily all right?" Sarah asks; she covers her mouth briefly from dust kicked up by the bus.

"She's fine," Miles says.

"Did you feed her like I said?"

"Yes. She's fine!" Miles says. "Come on, let's go. We don't need to stand around on the highway all day."

He heads down the ditch to the woods trail. Sarah knows to step in his tracks—so it appears like a single set of footprints—until they're safely into the woods. There, it's a twenty-minute walk through the late-summer woods. The aspens have yellow leaves, and a few scarlet maples stand out against dusty green pines. Forests used to scare her.

"How are we going to do this in winter?" Sarah asks. "Get to the highway, I mean."

"On snowshoes or skis," Miles says.

"Great," Sarah mutters.

"Or maybe by snowmobile," Miles adds.

"We're getting a snowmobile?" Sarah asks.

Miles shrugs. "I hope."

As soon Sarah comes in sight above the cabin, Emily starts to *"Baaaack, baaack!"* She jumps up and down as if she's on springs. Emily goes crazy on her rope, and races around in tight circles until she winds herself against her tree. Then she reverses directions and unwinds herself like a runaway top. Sarah laughs and grabs her as she races by. They tumble onto the grass in a heap of girl arms and goat legs.

"Did Miles feed you?" Sarah murmurs. She feels Emily's udders, which are tight with milk.

"Yes, I fed her," Miles says with annoyance, and heads over to the sawmill shed.

She holds Emily by her long ears and looks into her pretty yellow eyes with their little dark bars for pupils. People have round pupils; goats have rectangular ones. Miles was the first to notice that (which was annoying), but Miles doesn't know where she likes to be scratched (right behind her stubby little horns), or what all of her little head butting and hopping gestures really mean.

"Sarah! You're home," her mother says. She comes around the corner of the cabin. From the dust, her black hair is streaked with gray, and Sarah has a sudden, scary image of her mother as an old woman.

"Yeah?" Sarah says.

"You survived day one of school!" her mother says.

"Barely," Sarah mutters.

"Hey, how was school?" Artie asks, appearing beside Nat and draping an arm around her. He, too, is covered in dust and looks twenty years older.

"Sorta like Willy Wonka's chocolate factory but without the chocolate," Sarah says, looking away.

"Welcome to the Machine," Miles calls out. He loves old Pink Floyd music.

"Did you meet anybody?" Nat inquires.

Sarah thinks first of Ray, then of Mackenzie and her gang. "Not really," she says. She thinks of the thin girl with dark eyes. "I have to milk Emily, and then she and I are heading down to the river for a swim," Sarah says. "A little privacy, all right?"

"Sure. And when you're done, Miles could use some help in the saw shack," her father says.

Sarah mumbles something she's lucky no one hears and goes to the cabin for the little milk pail. Miles has made a small wooden stanchion and platform inside the corral; and when Sarah returns, Emily is standing on the boards, head between the two vertical boards, ready to be milked.

"What a good Emily!" Sarah gives her a treat—a

handful of grass—and then loops the short rope around the stanchion's top. The vertical boards squeeze—but do not pinch—Emily's neck and ensure that she doesn't jerk or jump and race off while Sarah is milking her. Sarah kneels and, with a wet cloth, washes Emily's two little teats; after that, in a downward pull, she strokes a squirt of milk from each one. That first squirt is to the side, to the ground; it's to remove any bacteria on the teat end or in the teat itself. Once that's done, Sarah hangs the little stainless steel pail on her left wrist and milks with her right hand. She always leans her forehead into the little valley between Emily's rib cage and her hip bone, a soft indentation, and closes her eyes as she works. Emily's chewing makes a faint, faraway rocking motion, and Sarah falls into the rhythm of milking: stroke, *tingy-ting*, stroke, *tingy-ting*.

Gradually the *tingy-ting* of milk hitting the bottom of the pail softens to *tungy-shush, tungy-shush*, and soon it's *shush-shush, shush-shush, shush-shush*.

Milking takes only five minutes. Soon they are done. Holding the pail handle tightly, she releases Emily—who hops away and races playfully about the corral.

"Yes, yes, yes," Sarah says. "I'll be right back—hang on."

She goes to the river and to Miles's homemade refrigerator, a wire cage weighed down by two stones, that sits in the cool water. Floating inside are two glass jars—former peanut butter jars—full of milk; for now Emily has more milk than they can drink in a day. Sarah pours the milk from the pail into two more clean jars and slips the warm ones into the cold river water and the cage. She makes sure to arrange the jars in order of freshness. They all drink goat's milk, which at first made her gag; it is yellower, heavier, and way thicker than regular milk. Now she is not sure she could drink cow's milk from a store.

After her chores are complete, she goes to get Emily for her daily outing. On the short leash, Emily hops and jumps—which always makes Sarah laugh—and they head to the river, Emily nipping off bites of thin grass along the way.

The warmth of the day has collected along the riverbank, and though it's now the first week of September, the water is still warm from the summer. She goes just around the bend, peeking back at the cabin to make sure no one can see, then hangs her towel on a branch. In her little changing stall she slips off her clothes. Skinny-dipping is something she could never do back in the suburbs; maybe it's one reward for living like the Swiss Family Robinson. Though when it gets cold, she might have to join a sports team so she can shower at school.

With Emily grazing along the bank, Sarah wades into the water until it's knee-deep, then lies down in the cool flow. Using a bar of soap, she washes the school cooties off her—soapy water curls away and disappears—then holds wide her arms and floats on her back. She closes her eyes as the river takes her a few yards, then she swims back upstream and does it again. Each time she floats downstream, she keeps her eyes closed a little longer, making a game of guessing which big tree she'll see when she opens them.

Emily grazes along, following her downstream. Soon they are out of sight of the cabin. There's a bend in the river, and a deeper pool where Miles catches fish; he doesn't like her swimming here because she scares them away, he says. She does it anyway.

The pool, about twenty feet wide and eight feet deep, is very cold at the bottom. As she paddles down, she opens her eyes. Several shadows—fish—dart away; she stays down as long as she can, inspecting the bottom, the smooth stones, a couple of crayfish with their whiskery noses and oversize pincers.

She surfaces, quietly, pretending she's a rare freshwater mermaid whom no human has ever seen, and then sinks down again. Stays under longer this time. She hears faint chirping noises, like faraway birds or maybe minnows calling to each other, warning about the mermaid. As she heads back to the glassy ceiling, the noises are louder. Emily! Emily bleating and splashing in the water, tangled in her rope. Onshore, creeping along toward Emily, is the old dog.

"Shoo! Go away!" Sarah shouts, bursting naked out of the water. The dog freezes. Then in a swirl of gray, he runs away, kicking up dust on the bank, taking long, limping strides. One of his hind legs is either short or broken. The dog is the same color as the brush into which he disappears.

Still wet, Sarah pulls on her clothes just as the whole family comes running down to the river.

"What happened?" Miles shouts, leading the way. He has his gun.

"I saw the dog on the bank," she says, untangling Emily's tether rope. "I thought he was going toward

Emily, but he wasn't."

"How do you know?" Miles presses.

"You sure it wasn't a wolf or something?" Nat asks.

"No. Just an old dog. He had a bad leg. He limped."

Miles kneels down to examine the dog's tracks. "It's been hanging around here."

Artie and Nat glance at each other. "Don't go so far downstream, all right?" Natalie says.

"So I'm supposed to take a bath where everybody can watch me?"

"That's not what I'm saying. Just stay a little closer, that's all."

After her parents and Miles are gone, she dries her hair. Emily is still trembling.

"He was just an old dog," Sarah says. "You're fine." Holding tightly to Emily's rope, she heads back to the cabin.

Emerging from the bushes, she pauses to stare at the shabby log cabin. The square little room that Miles is adding. The dusty path. The tumbledown sawmill shed. She drops to her knees and hugs Emily. Then her eyes catch sight of Miles's shotgun leaning against the cabin wall. She walks over, picks it up; it's heavier than she imagined, and the curve of its stock feels good. She hoists it; it sits awkwardly on her arm at first, then settles comfortably against her shoulder.

"Want to shoot it?" Miles says from behind her.

"No!" she says quickly, and puts down the gun.

"Wouldn't hurt you to learn," Miles said.

"Forget it," Sarah says. "I'm never shooting a gun."

CHAPTER EIGHT

MILES

RETURNING FROM HUNTING, MILES LOOKS up at the hazy yellow sky. It's almost ten A.M. His mother is in the yard. "Is Dad up yet?" he asks.

"Sort of," she says.

Inside the cabin, Miles's father is slumped forward over his breakfast coffee.

"You ready to work?" Miles says.

"Absolutely, son. Raring to go," Artie says, taking out one earbud. "Just tell me what to do."

It's supposed to funny, but his father doesn't smile. Here in the north woods he's a fish out of water. That, and being humiliated by the biker family back at Birch Bay, has broken something inside him. He looks older and smaller these days.

"Home remodeling 101 starts in five," Miles says.

"Be with you as soon as I finish my coffee," Artie says, holding up one of Mr. Kurz's tin cups.

Outside, in the hazy sunlight, Miles sets to work on the addition—the "kids' bedroom." It's a lean-to, ten feet by ten feet, on the side of the cabin. The roof joists slant down to the vertical stud walls. Mr. Kurz's cabin is made from hand-hewed logs, the adze marks still visible on the thick, gray wood. The Newell addition is built from boards found in the various lumber piles.

Artie soon appears. "Tell me what to do," he says, kicking at some boards.

"General carpentry," Miles says. "A new career for you if the music thing doesn't work out."

It's a gesture to his father, a joke—his Shawnee Kingston Band is a well-known group in the Midwest— but Artie pauses to stare at his gloved hands. "Don't let me cut off any of my fingers."

"I won't," Miles says.

They start the work together by sorting boards. Mr. Kurz had his own sawmill, with a gas-powered engine (rusted and dead). Around it are stacks of graying planks, boards, and slabs—some with rotted wood on top but with solid ones deeper in the pile. Behind the big, rusty circular saw blade is a mound of dust. Like the wood, it is gray, but only on top; if you kick away the crust, the sawdust is yellow and piney-fragrant underneath.

"Here's a couple of good ones," Artie says, and begins to drag them out.

"Too thick," Miles says. "We need boards, not planks, for the roof."

They work in silence, carrying boards together, one of them on each end, as they stage them beside the skeleton frame.

"Your mother told me she met some family in a canoe," Artie says.

"Got caught, you mean. I wish she'd pay more attention."

"She's a city girl. Like me," Artie says with a glance to Miles.

"Well, we're country people now," Miles answers.

"More like forest people," Artie says, pausing to look around.

"But forest people with plenty of food," Miles says. "If there's any time to be off the grid, it's now." He motions to his father to pay attention to their work.

"True," Artie says. "But try not to be so tough on them," he adds, meaning Nat and Sarah. "They're doing the best they can."

"We all have to be on guard all the time," Miles says. "The minute we let down our guard, something bad will happen."

His father stops. "You know, Miles, it's good that you're protective," he says. "But I don't want you to obsess on our safety."

"Somebody has to," Miles shoots back.

His father purses his lips as if about to say something. Instead, he lifts another board.

"Remember our trip up here from the city?" Miles continues. "Our ninety-dollar breakfast at the Golden Arches? Those dudes who chased us at the Dairy Queen?"

"Yes," his father says, "but we have to believe that most people are basically well-intentioned."

"You sound like Anne Frank," Miles says, "and we all know what happened to her."

Artie grunts and lifts his end of the stack of three boards. They drop the boards onto the pile and keep working. With hammers, they nail boards horizontally onto the vertical studs and make a rising exterior wall.

After a while, his father straightens up to wipe sweat from his face. He looks at their work. "Aren't board walls going to be cold this winter?"

"We're going to insulate the walls," Miles says.

"How? With what?" Artie asks.

"The old way," Miles says.

Artie scratches his head and looks around.

"Don't worry, I'll show you," Miles answers.

After an hour they take a short break and sit down. They inspect their work, which is most of the outside wall. "Now we have to do the same thing on the inside wall," Miles says.

"That will leave an air space," Artie says.

"Exactly," Miles says.

"How are we going to get insulation inside there?"

"You'll see," Miles says.

"And what about windows?" Artie asks.

Miles pauses. He actually hadn't thought about that. "Windows let in the cold," he answers.

"We—you and Sarah—need a window," Artie says.

"Okay, okay," Miles says.

It's a half hour of work, but he boxes in a square big enough to escape through if they had to.

"I still don't see how we can insulate the space now," Artie says.

"Here," Miles says, handing his father a shovel and an old pail.

"What's this for?"

Miles points to the sawdust pile. "We have plenty of insulation!"

Atop a homemade ladder, with his parents providing a bucket brigade, he pours sawdust down into the channels between the walls. Bucket after bucket. As it sifts down, it fills all the cracks.

"What's for supper?" Miles says later.

"Chili and rice," Nat says.

"Veggie chili, I suppose," Miles says.

"Yes, sorry," Nat says.

"When it gets colder, we're going to eat venison," Miles says.

"Not me!" Nat says.

"We'll see," Miles says to his mom.

"Forget it," she says.

"Remember when you hit that deer with your BMW?"

"Please. That was horrible and expensive."

"I'm just saying—if somebody had eaten that deer, you wouldn't have hit it with your car."

"Well, we don't have a car, so no need to worry about hitting a deer," she answers.

"Speaking of which, we'll need a snowmobile for this winter," Miles says.

"Huh?" Nat says.

"A snowmobile? I thought you wanted to be green," Artie says.

"There's green, and there's getting to town once a week when the snow comes," Miles says.

"Good point. I guess your motorbike won't work," Nat asks. Miles convinced his parents to spring for one not long after they arrived at Mr. Kurz's cabin.

"Not in deep snow," Miles says. *I've seen it snow at least a little every month of the year up north. Some winters it was halfway up the cabin wall. But snow is a good thing in deep winter. Keeps the ground warm—the critters, too. Deer curl up to sleep. Partridge fly right into it and bury themselves for the night. Sleep like babies. . . .*

Artie looks at Nat. "A snowmobile might be a good idea—especially for emergencies," he offers. It's the first time he's actually made a suggestion or had an opinion.

"Like a run to town for pizza," Miles adds.

They continue lifting pails of sawdust. Working together is something they never did back home in the suburbs. There, everybody was always heading off in a different direction.

"By the way, I saw that dog," Nat says.

"Where?" Miles quickly asks.

She gestures to the edge of the woods. "He was just sitting there, watching us. When I looked at him, he got all scared and disappeared. I took some scraps up there for him to eat—he looked really hungry."

Miles kicks the ground. "Do not feed him! The last thing we need around here is a stray dog."

"Sorry," Nat says quickly. "But I couldn't help myself. He's so sad looking."

"He's a wild dog. He could be dangerous."

"Maybe we could tame him. Make him a watchdog," Artie says.

"I'm the watchdog," Miles says.

CHAPTER NINE

SARAH

FRIDAY AFTER SCHOOL, SARAH DOES not take the bus home. She has been invited over to Mackenzie's house to spend the night. Sarah was not wild about the whole idea, but staying in a house with actual plumbing helped her decide.

First, however, she has to wait until Mackenzie is done with after-school tennis practice. She watches while the girls' team volleys back and forth. Very few of them have any kind of follow-through on their shots, and the coach, an older woman teacher perched on a stool, either doesn't notice or doesn't care.

"Come on, Sarah, want to hit a few?" Mackenzie teases.

"No thanks, it's not really my game," Sarah calls back.

"Come on, Sarah," Rachel adds, clearly dying to take a breather.

"Why not?" Mackenzie says. "There's an extra racket in the bag."

Sarah shrugs. "I'm not really dressed right." She has on her jeans.

"Just a couple of volleys," Mackenzie says.

Sarah stretches briefly, then picks up the racket. She spins it in her hands, taps its head on concrete to test its heft, then plucks at the nylon mesh to test its tension.

"Okay, here goes nothing," Sarah says. Out of habit from playing with Nat and Miles on their home court, she flips a dead ball off the concrete, then tosses it up. Her serve feels good—she has a momentary sensation of being home. Mackenzie strokes the ball back to her. Sarah ranges left and returns the volley. She remembers to be clumsy—at least in her footwork—but her arm does not obey. With a smooth, level sweep, she returns the ball.

"Hey, that was nice!" Rachel calls. She stops to stare.

Mackenzie returns the ball, harder this time.

Sarah goes right and turns over a nice forearm stroke that Mackenzie just barely manages to return. It's an easy play for Sarah; she could nail it in the corner where Mackenzie would never reach it, but she pretends to stumble and draws up short.

"Sorry!" she calls to Mackenzie.

"Hey, that's all right. I've been playing for years," Mackenzie says.

They do a few more volleys, during which Sarah makes sure to miss a few more shots. "That's it for me," Sarah calls, and walks off the court. As she returns the racket to a big gym bag, the tennis coach walks over.

"What are you doing?" she says. She is not smiling.

"Uh, putting away the racket?"

"No. Out there." The coach nods toward the court.

"Sorry! I know I'm not on the team, but they asked me to volley."

"Not that. I mean, pretending that you can't play."

Sarah is silent.

The teacher allows a faint smile and takes off her sunglasses. She has steely blue eyes that penetrate Sarah's gaze. "You play, don't you?"

Sarah shrugs. "A little."

"So why not come out for the team?"

"Sorry, can't. I have to go home after school."

"What's your name, by the way?"

"Sarah. Sarah Newell."

"And you're a transfer student, right?"

The coach is trying, but Sarah feels trapped. Vulnerable. She's starting to think like Miles. She nods.

"So where did you move from?"

"Park Rapids area. I'm on open enrollment."

"Great," the coach says. "Good to have you here. I know a tennis player when I see one."

Sarah glances away. Mackenzie is watching them even as she strokes and volleys.

"Maybe you and I can hit some balls someday—by ourselves, I mean," the coach says. "Just for fun."

"Sure. Okay." Anything to end this conversation.

"So, don't be a stranger, all right?"

Sarah nods, then hurries off to the side, where she hunkers down in the corner, draws up her knees, and watches the bright balls dart back and forth.

That night she goes home with Mackenzie. The Phelpses' house, with a brick front and three-car garage, is big for Bemidji but would be a loser house back in her suburb. They go in through the garage door; inside, filling up two of the empty stalls, are several dozen five-gallon red plastic gas jugs. They're arranged in tidy rows, like a secret garden.

"My dad," Mackenzie says with a shrug. "He knows this gas guy."

"But you have a Blue Star," Sarah says. It just pops out.

"Yeah, but we still have to look out for ourselves, he says."

Inside the house, Mackenzie drops down to hug a yapping little white dog. "Hi, Mitzy!"

"How was practice today?" her father asks immediately. He's a thick, balding guy who still has on his tie from work.

"So-so," Mackenzie says with a shrug. She drops her duffel bag—*plop!*—on the floor.

"Did you ask the coach about playing some of the high school girls to make sure you're being challenged?" he inquires. He ignores Sarah.

"She said 'Maybe,'" Mackenzie replies.

Sarah stands behind Mackenzie like a knob on the side door. Mitzy is sniffing and sniffing her shoes—and starts to growl.

"Stop that, Mitzy!" Mackenzie says. "Whatever is the matter with you?"

"Clearly you're not being assertive enough," her father responds. "I'll call your coach this week."

"So," Mackenzie's mother interrupts. "Mackenzie tells me she's met a new friend."

Sarah smiles shyly.

"Hi there, Sarah," she says. "I'm Jane. This is Mackenzie's dad, Bill. Please, come in."

"Hi, Mr. and Mrs. Phelps," Sarah says as she shakes hands with each of them

"Just Bill and Jane," Sarah's mom says with a smile. Bill Phelps has thick fingers with hair on the backs of them. Jane is tidy and fit, a woman who has time to work out and get her short blond hair done. It's shiny and looks stiff.

"And where are you from?" Bill asks. He doesn't smile as easily as Mackenzie's mother.

Sarah goes through her open enrollment, school transfer thing. She's getting better and better at lying.

"Do you do sports?" he asks.

"Not really," Sarah answers.

"You'd be good at tennis," Mackenzie says. "You should try it."

Bill Phelps gives his daughter a what-a-dumb-thing-to-say look. Mackenzie quickly looks down. Then he laughs as if Mackenzie was joking. "It's not like you can just pick up a racket and play," he says to Sarah. "All my kids grew up hitting tennis balls. It's why they're so good—right, honey?"

Mackenzie doesn't answer.

"And you live outside of town?" Jane asks Sarah—as if to change the subject.

"That's right."

"On a lake?" Jane asks.

"Yes." It's sort of true.

"That must be nice," she says with a glance toward her husband. "There are some beautiful lake homes around here."

"Do you have a big house?" Mackenzie asks.

"Not really," Sarah says, pretending mock embarrassment. "It's more of a summer place."

As dinner proceeds, there is less focus on Sarah. Sitting at an actual dinner table with soft chairs gradually makes Sarah weepy. To get a grip she says, "The hot dish is excellent." Actually it's long on cheese and short on meat, but she feels as if she needs to say something polite.

Mackenzie's mom is pleased. "Thank you, dear." She passes the bowl back to Sarah. "Mackenzie just never eats enough. It's so nice to have a hungry girl at the table."

"What lake do you live on again?" Bill asks abruptly.

"Actually, it's the river," Sarah says. "The Mississippi."

"I see," he says, nodding. "Judge Lawrence and his wife have a big house out on the Mississippi. Do you know them?"

"Sorry, no," Sarah answers.

"Excellent judge. Great people. Sound family values."

"Have you found a church yet? A congregation here in town?" Jane asks Sarah.

"Not yet. We're still—sort of—getting settled," Sarah says.

"Well, there are many nice church groups in town," Mackenzie's mother says. "You'll have to visit our church—it's the biggest one, just east of town?"

Sarah nods. "I'll mention it to my parents."

"And what do they do?" Bill asks. Jane shoots him a slightly annoyed glance.

"My father's . . . retired. My mother is a literary agent, so she can work from home. From anywhere, really."

"We'd love to meet them. Do you have brothers or sisters?" Jane asks cheerfully.

"I'm an only child," Sarah says, then take a big gulp of her milk—and scrunches up her face. This milk tastes thin and watery, and maybe it's her imagination, but she thinks she can taste chemicals.

Mackenzie's mother frowns. "That must be lonely. Mackenzie has two older brothers in college. They were both all-state in tennis," she adds. She scoops more of the casserole onto Mackenzie's plate. Mackenzie makes a face and pushes away her plate.

"In any case, we'd love to meet your parents!" Jane says again.

The Friday-night football game is preceded by a giant Zamboni-like machine, really a huge vacuum cleaner that makes steady passes up and down the field. It leaves strips of brighter green grass in its wake. The dust is bad lately. Coughing up and down the bleachers has a ragged rhythm like acorns falling onto a roof. However, on this small-town Friday night with football under the lights, the high school band thumps loudly, the cheerleaders bounce and cartwheel, and the crowd cheers—though voices are muffled behind dust masks. Sarah follows Mackenzie to a group of girls high up in the bleachers. "It's important to see over the back so we know who's coming and going," Mackenzie explains.

Just before the game starts, Sarah looks over her shoulder and down. Something just made her look. Ray is staring up at her. His earbuds are in, but he's focused on her.

He waves.

She swallows, then discreetly lifts her chin.

He is holding two bags of popcorn, one of which he holds up to her.

Sarah turns quickly back to the other girls.

"What?" Mackenzie asks. She has major radar.

"Nothing." Sarah sits for a moment. "Actually, are the bathrooms down there?"

"Somebody go with Sarah and show her the can," Mackenzie says, and there is laughter.

"I will, I will," chirp a couple of voices, including Rachel's.

"No—you'll miss the kickoff. I can find it myself." With that, Sarah trots down the metal steps just as the national anthem starts: perfect timing, as none of the girls get up and follow her.

Behind the grandstand bleachers, Ray is nowhere to be seen. Which is fine, because Rachel, hand over her heart and singing the anthem, is looking over her shoulder and down at Sarah.

Sarah waves and continues toward the concession stand and restroom building.

Ray is leaning against a large wooden post, waiting for her. His ever-present sketch pad is tucked behind his belt; a pencil point pokes out of the dark hair over his right ear. From behind his back, he whips out two little brown bags and holds out one to her. "Popcorn?"

"Maybe," Sarah says. "Though how do I know it doesn't have some sort of date drug?"

Ray grins. "Here's mine; we'll switch."

"That old switch-the-popcorn-bag trick," Sarah says as she takes his.

They stand munching their popcorn like crazy so they don't have to talk.

"So where are all your friends tonight?" Sarah asks.

Ray shrugs. "They're not big football fans."

"So what brings you here?"

"Well. To be honest . . ." Suddenly Ray gags—then coughs and expels a white bullet of popcorn. "Jeez, sorry!" He covers his mouth, and his face reddens.

"The old choke-on-the-popcorn trick," Sarah says.

Ray's dark eyes shine; they make Sarah's face feel warm.

"No kilt tonight?" She glances down at his jeans.

"It gets cold later," Ray says, "if you know what I mean."

"Let's not go there," Sarah says. It's her turn to grin stupidly and look away.

"Actually, I wear the kilt just to annoy Mr. James, the school principal. Drives him crazy."

"How so?"

"Enforcing the school dress codes is his life's ambition. He called me in right away the first day of school about my kilt and threatened to send me home. But I was way ahead of him—I had the papers," Ray says.

"Papers?"

"If you have a Scottish family name, there's a particular plaid that belongs to your clan. I had the list that proved it, so he had to let me go. But he was steamed, let me tell you."

Sarah glances over her shoulder toward the bleachers. Rays starts munching popcorn again. "So tell me about your family," she says.

"Pretty generic," Ray says. "One older brother. My

mom's an artist—which is sort of where I got hooked on drawing, I guess—and my dad's a nurse at the hospital. I work there, too, about twenty hours a week."

"So you're an artist and a doctor?" Sarah teases.

"I wish. My dad got me a janitor's job. I'm one of the swing-shift guys who do floors. What about your family?"

She gives him the short version: transfer student on open enrollment, her family's summer place "on the lake," a phrase that everybody in Minnesota understands. "My mom's an editor and a literary agent, and my dad's a musician," she says.

"A musician? Cool," Ray says.

"Sort of a musician," she says quickly. "More like wants to be a musician. Someday."

"What does he play?"

She hesitates a second. "Piano," she says.

Ray nods. "My mom's a sculptor. She makes these wild things out of found material. She won't use anything new—it has to be thrown-away stuff."

"Cool," Sarah says.

They're standing really close now.

"I'd better get back," Sarah says.

The skin on Ray's forehead bunches. "Before you do,

tell me again why you hang out with Mackenzie?"

"Why do you hang out with your friends?" she replies.

"Mackenzie's not your friend. The only friend Mackenzie has is Mackenzie."

"I've gotta go. Really."

"See you in school?" Ray says.

"I guess."

"What I meant was will you talk to me in school?"

"Sure," Sarah says evasively.

"No, I mean *talk* talk. Like we are now."

"Sure. That is, if I have no aftereffects from the popcorn you gave me." They hug briefly, clumsily, and then Sarah hurries away.

Back in the bleachers, Mackenzie is overly focused on the game.

"There goes Django!" Rachel says as a receiver races for a pass—and gathers it in. The crowd cheers. Django breaks loose for a few yards but is tackled; he goes down in a pile of players and a faint cloud of dust.

"What's the score?" Sarah says brightly.

Mackenzie is silent. Then she turns to Sarah. "Were you talking to that creepy Ray?"

Sarah clears her throat. "Yeah. Sort of. We were both

getting some popcorn, so, you know, it's not like I could avoid him."

"Right," Mackenzie says flatly. Her eyes turn back to the game.

"Want some?" Sarah asks, holding out the bag.

Mackenzie ignores the popcorn. "Ray O'Keefe is from this really crazy family. They live in this little house right in town. His dad bikes everywhere, even in winter, and his mom is this old hippie or something. They're, like, totally poor."

Back at Mackenzie's house they get ready for bed. Mackenzie's room is nearly half the size of the cabin and has its own bathroom. Mackenzie and Rachel go in to brush their teeth, and Sarah goes to wash in the hall bathroom. She takes her time, washing her face and then running the warm water over her hands for a few extra minutes, savoring the luxury of indoor plumbing. Of hot water.

Heading back to Mackenzie's room, she pauses in the hallway before a wall full of family photographs, all framed. Mackenzie's brothers in their letter jackets. Mackenzie with her tennis racket. The entire family posed together in the backyard, smiling and happy. All the pictures look so . . . normal. So BV.

When Sarah returns to the bedroom, Mackenzie and Rachel are sprawled on the queen-size bed poring over their sixth-grade yearbook. "Come on, Sarah," Mackenzie says. "This will be very educational for you." Rachel giggles. Mackenzie starts flipping pages and pointing to pictures; her mood has improved.

"That's Dylan," she says, pointing to a skinny boy with his hair in his eyes. "He was a total loser last year; but he sits behind me in algebra this year, and I noticed that he got cute over the summer."

"I always thought he was cute," says Rachel, staring at the picture.

"Really, Rachel," Mackenzie says. "You have such low expectations."

"And there's Kara Lindberg," Rachel says. "Remember her?"

"Ick," Mackenzie says with a shudder. "She and her family came here last fall from Colorado. Her parents lost their jobs after the volcanoes and then their house was foreclosed on, so they had to move."

"That's horrible," Sarah says quickly.

Mackenzie shrugs. "They were camping in the state park here. She had to shower in the school locker room."

"No way!" Sarah says, as if that was totally disgusting.

"Definitely a Traveler," Rachel says. "And we could tell anyway, because Traveler kids always tried to charge their cell phones at school."

"Remember how Sharelle 'accidentally' stepped on Kara's phone and smashed it?" Mackenzie says.

Rachel laughs wildly.

Mackenzie wrinkles her nose. "Anyway, there were lots of icky homeless people from the cities who just showed up thinking they could freeload on all of us who actually live here. I'm really glad they passed that law so they all had to leave."

"Me, too," Rachael says. "Most of them smelled funny."

"They should never have put Kara in the yearbook," Mackenzie says.

"For sure not!" Rachel says.

Sarah fakes a yawn. "I'm tired," she says, flopping onto her sleeping bag.

"Me, too," Mackenzie says. "And I have a tennis lesson in the morning." She flicks the light switch as the girls snuggle down under comforters and into sleeping bags. They giggle for a while longer about Dylan and Django and other cute boys and then, slowly, the room grows quiet. Eventually Sarah hears Mackenzie's deep, rhythmic breathing and Rachel's tiny snoring sounds. But she is wide-awake.

Icky homeless people. That would pretty much be her.

CHAPTER TEN

MILES

ON SATURDAY MILES TAKES HIS mother to town on his Kawasaki motorbike. It's his second trip; he had to pick up Sarah from her stupid sleepover. For some reason he wasn't supposed to arrive at the Phelps house, so they met downtown. But Saturdays are good for riding. There are more people around that day—the grocery stores are busier, and there's more traffic—which makes it easier to blend in with the locals.

"We'll get groceries on the way home," Miles says over his shoulder and through his bandana.

"Okay," his mother says, her voice muffled against

his back. She hangs on for dear life; Miles knows that she hates the dirt bike, but she's a businesswoman and not dumb. The bike is the perfect solution for now: It gets close to a hundred miles to a gallon of gas and has knobby, off-road tires for escaping into the woods if needed. A dirt bike and a gun: two things he never would have owned back in the suburbs.

On the highway, the bike leaves a dark stripe in the pale ash. Pumice dust rolls up behind them like a contrail of jet exhaust in the sky. He can only see gray in the little rearview mirror—not that there is much traffic to worry about. Soon the nose of a pickup grows in the oval glass of his mirror, and its rumbling V-8 comes on fast. Miles veers onto the shoulder to let it pass. When the truck streams by, the highway in front is gone—lost in a rolling, gray dust cloud. Disorientation hits—like a pilot losing which way is up—and he concentrates on keeping his handlebars straight. When the air doesn't clear, he looks straight down beside his right boot and picks up the seam where the shoulder meets the main highway. A line, somewhere between gray and brown—enough to keep them on the road— unwinds ahead. Gradually the wider highway returns to view. Behind, his mother coughs and presses her head tighter against his back.

He takes the back route into town, passing the high school and the entrance to a juvenile lockup. He goes over a railroad crossing and up a grade to the traffic light by the post office, where they pick up their mail once a week.

PLEASE REMOVE DUST MASKS AT THE DOOR, a sign reads. Miles waits on the motorbike while his mother goes in. She's out in two minutes, thumbing through a handful of letters and clutching a couple of packages—book manuscripts probably—under her other arm.

"Let's roll," Miles says. "You can look at that stuff later."

"'That stuff' is how we make a living, thank you very much," his mother says.

"How you do that is a mystery to me," Miles says as he stashes her mail in the right-side saddlebag. His mother playfully squeezes his rib cage as they motor off. It's one more thing they would never have done in the burbs: get his mother to ride on the back of a dirt bike.

The next stop is the library, a modern, one-story building with outthrust roof angles where Nat does her e-mail and internet thing once a week, plus charges Artie's iPod.

"See you here later," she says.

Miles nods, then chains the Kawasaki to a bike rack, after which he walks over to the Alternative Education Center. It's a low brick building open on Saturdays, which only makes sense. And that's what he likes about the AEC—there are no bells. No principals.

Inside the waiting area the old couch is occupied by two girls, one with a lot of piercings and raccoon-style black eye makeup, the other with a real baby under a small blanket. "Hey," Miles says.

The young mom smiles tiredly. She's about Miles's age and pretty in a skinny, pale kind of way; it's as if all of her physical powers went into her baby, which makes smacking and sucking noises under the blanket. As she shifts the baby, the white top of one breast curves upward. Miles quickly looks away (the dark-eyed chick gives him a disgusted look). Carrying his packet, he slides past her to the check-in desk.

"Mr. L in?" he asks.

"Sure am!" a man's voice calls from a cubicle just beyond. A head pops up, bald on top but with a thin gray ponytail behind. "Be with you in a few minutes, Miles."

The teachers here are cooler than at regular school,

too, ones such as Mr. Lewandowski, who didn't fit into public school—"The Machine," as Mr. L called it.

Rather than hang with the girls in the lobby, Miles heads to the bathroom, where he takes a long time on the toilet. Afterward he spends time at the sink washing up all over, including his armpits, which were, he has to admit, a tiny bit rank. Clean, he reemerges, ready for a second chance with the girls on the couch. The young mom and her baby are gone, but the pierced girl glares at him as if daring him to say something. He sits down anyway. Looks through a gummy magazine.

"I hate this," the girl says suddenly.

"What is *this*?" Miles asks pleasantly.

"Everything," she mutters.

"Let's turn that frown upside down!" Miles says. It's supposed to come out funny—a parody of an overly cheerful host on a kids' television show—but it clanks.

The girl stares at him. "Are you insane?"

"Ah, I don't think so," Miles says. "But you never know."

That clanks, too. The girl crosses her arms across her chest and looks out the window. Miles is trying to think of something not insane to say when Mr. Lewandowski calls his name.

"Sorry, got to go," he says to the pierced girl.

She does not reply.

"So, how are things?" Mr. Lewandowski asks. They shake hands, and Miles sits down.

"No problems, really," Miles says.

Mr. Lewandowski leans back in a creaky chair. "Your stuff is all good—math especially."

"Thanks."

They take a few minutes and go through his packet, after which Mr. Lewandowski hands Miles the next one. This school proceeds at the student's pace; and since Miles is all caught up, they have time to BS about the state of the world. "I try to remain optimistic," Mr. L says as he kicks back, "because, hey, what's the alternative?" He laughs.

It takes Miles a second to get the joke.

Back at the library, Miles finds that his mother is still waiting for a computer terminal. She holds up her hands and shrugs, so he skulks along the magazine shelves. He picks up a Fun FAQs About Volcanoes sheet that has been scrawled upon and defaced. It's good to see that some kids—by the looks of the handwriting—are on guard against stupidity. He glances around the library but sees only adults and little stumblers plus a couple of crying babies.

He scores a well-thumbed *Popular Mechanics*. He reads and people watches over the top of his magazine. The library patrons have some rough edges; their clothes smell like dogs and wood smoke. A mother and her three squirming kids check out a stack of DVDs. The bestseller display is picked mostly clean. Audio books are mostly gone, too. In the far corner there's a big-screen television in a small room, with headsets for listening. On the silent screen, a rolling banner beneath two talking heads reads "Climate conditions improving: full summer growing season predicted." Right. That's what they said at the beginning of the summer, and barely a seed sprouted. If adults obsessed about the weather before the volcanoes, now the weather report is the only topic. Miles is tempted to listen, but the television room is crowded and warm, and anyway, he has given up on television. There's no good news, and if there is, who knows if it's true?

A fat woman gets up from a computer terminal. The librarian calls out, "Natalie?"

His mother hands Miles her purse and the mail for safekeeping, and takes a seat at computer station number four.

The woman librarian glances at the sign-up sheet. "It's Natalie—?" she asks. She wants a last name.

"Just Natalie," Miles's mother says cheerfully, and turns to her work.

The librarian pauses, then moves on. Computer terminals have a one-hour limit, and his mother is just getting up to speed—she types faster than a woodpecker pecks—when the reference librarian returns with the clipboard.

"Excuse me," the librarian says to Nat.

Miles lowers his magazine.

"Yes?" Nat asks. There's annoyance in her voice.

"Do you have some form of identification?" the woman asks.

Nat is silent. People turn to stare. "I'm sorry, say again?" Miles's mother asks the librarian.

"ID," the librarian repeats. "A driver's license. Something."

"And why would I need that?" Nat asks, still keeping her smile, though it has slipped big-time. "I come here all the time."

"We have . . . orders. Instructions to serve our local community first. If you live outside of Beltrami County—if you're traveling through—you'll have to give up the terminal if there are local people waiting."

"Who says I live outside the county?" Nat says.

Miles glances around. To the side, a scrawny guy in clothes two sizes too big looks away.

"I'm not at liberty to answer that," the librarian says. She looks toward the scrawny guy, whose cover is blown.

He swallows. "What she's saying is you're either local or you're not," the guy says to Miles's mother. He stays back as if to keep an escape route open behind him.

Nat gives him a glance as if he's a passing fruit fly. Miles slips behind a row of tall bookshelves—the stacks—and glides up behind the guy. "You got a problem?" Miles says, making his voice low and weird.

The guy flinches and turns to Miles, who puffs himself up as tall as he can. It gives him an inch on the little man.

The guy's eyes go to Miles's wind-blown hair, his dusty red bandana. He swallows. "Not really," he says.

"Oh, there you are, son. I thought I'd lost you," Miles's mother says with very fake cheerfulness.

"I wuz over dere readin' the magazines," Miles says. He makes his voice sound like he's seriously abnormal.

"Good," she says. "Why don't you go on back there and sit in a chair until I'm ready, all right?" She uses her talking-to-a-child voice.

"All right, den," Miles says.

Nat turns back to the librarian; it takes his mother a second to find her groove again—but only a second. "Anyway, do you realize what you're asking?"

The librarian stares. "Yes. I'm asking for identification."

"The library is the last place in America where people should be asked for their ID," Nat says. Her voice rises.

Miles lingers nearby. He's not at all sure where this is going.

"Well, these are really not *my* instructions," the librarian says. "The governor himself—"

"Governor, schmovernor!" Nat says, rising from her chair to her full five feet two inches. "I know a few things about freedom of information. Just because we have an environmental crisis doesn't mean we have to have a police state!"

The librarian lets out a half hiccup sound; people all around stare, which doesn't bother Nat. She can do confrontations.

"You show me the rule where I have to show you my ID," Nat continues, getting up in the librarian's face. "I want to see it!"

"Excuse me! Excuse me! Is there some trouble here?" a stocky older man says. He's a shaved-head dude wearing a tie. An in-charge kind of guy.

"Yes, there is," Nat says.

"I only asked to see her identification," the woman librarian explains to her boss.

The tie guy pauses. "Technically, we really don't need to do that," he says to the librarian.

The woman's face begins to redden.

"You're thinking of our community first, which we all appreciate," he says calmly, and pats her arm. "But we don't need identification unless she wants to get a library card."

"She didn't put down her last name," the woman librarian says.

The head librarian does not hesitate. "Our patron here—"

"Natalie," Miles's mother says.

"—is free to be just 'Natalie,'" he continues. "We don't need to know any more about her than that, and she is welcome to use the library and all its resources."

Miles is impressed. The librarian, behind his lame tie and bald head, is a tough guy. He hasn't bought into the whole "Travelers" thing, the restricted-movements law.

"We shouldn't ignore government orders," the woman librarian says, stiffening her back.

"Of course we shouldn't," the older man says. "But the American public library takes its real direction from the United States Constitution, and all the rights and freedoms afforded therein."

This guy talks like a Founding Father—he should be wearing a white wig—and he's Miles's new hero.

After the woman librarian huffs away, Nat goes back to work, and gawkers stop watching, but it's not much of a victory. Later, on the way out of the library, Miles and his mother get more than their fair share of stares.

"Could you dial it back just a little next time?" Miles murmurs to his mother as he unlocks the chain.

"That was the last straw," Nat says, getting her back up again. "Imagine! Having to show ID in a library!"

"Yeah, well, the larger idea is not to call attention to ourselves."

She blinks and turns to him. "Says the son who ain't right in the head. Where did *that* come from?"

"It just . . . came," Miles says, holding back a grin.

"You scared even me!" his mother said.

Miles kicks over the engine, and they climb aboard. "Hang on," he says, and she does, tighter than ever.

Their next stop is the walk-up Wells Fargo ATM. Miles stays to the side, out of range of the little video eyeball above the keypad. His mother steps up and does her thing. The machine hums and clicks, and spits out cash.

"I've been thinking," Miles says.

"Worrying, you mean," his mother says as she tucks away the cash.

"We should stop using these machines," Miles says.

"I thought the idea was to save our stash at the cabin," Nat says, throwing a leg over the rear of the Kawasaki.

Bankers are not your friends. People learned that during the Depression. If there's a chance to steal your money, they will. How do you think they got so much money in the first place? The best way is cash on the barrelhead. And never keep it all in one place.

"Right," Miles says. "But the more we use a cash card, the more they know we're here."

"'They.' 'Them,'" his mother says, mimicking his voice. "Using an ATM is not a crime."

"No," Miles says, "but it leaves tracks. Electronic tracks. We're supposed to be living in Wayzata, not here."

"There is no 'here,'" Nat says, poking him playfully in the ribs as she gets on the bike. "We don't even have an address."

Next stop is the grocery store on the south side of town. Miles chains the Kawasaki to a light pole and goes in with his mother, if only to get his fair share of doom and gloom. The grocery store—the biggest in town—has lots of empty shelves. COMING SOON! and SHIPMENT DELAYED stickers decorate the open spaces. Other shelves have cleverly arranged cans of corn and boxes of cereal to disguise the fact that the space is less than half full. But there is way more food here than there was in Minneapolis.

An old man and his wife drift along the aisle, with a few scattered cans in the bottom of their grocery cart. "Never thought I'd see the day," he mutters.

"Yes, dear," she says automatically.

"You'd think we were in Russia," he says.

"Yes, dear."

"This is what happens when the Democrats take over," he says.

"You can't blame Democrats for the volcanoes, dear," she says pleasantly.

The produce section is vacant except for red potatoes and some rubbery-looking cucumbers. LIMIT: TEN POUNDS POTATOES PER WEEK! MUST SHOW COUPON!" a sign reads over the potatoes. Nat gestures, and Miles lifts a sack into their cart. In Dairy Products there is not a lot of milk but plenty of butter and cheese; in the meat section there is pork but very little beef.

"I could go for a major steak," Nat says, "a sixteen-ounce prime rib au jus."

"I thought you were a vegetarian," Miles says. "You and Goat Girl."

"Sarah," his mother says, then adds, "Hey, I'm only human. Just having a flashback to my unhealthy days as a carnivore."

"Some meat wouldn't hurt you," Miles said.

"I think it actually might," she says. "My stomach would freak."

"What else is on our list?" Miles says as they keep moving through the half-empty store.

"Romaine lettuce. Strawberries. Kiwis. Mangoes. Peaches," his mothers says, pretending to look at a list.

"Yeah, right," Miles says, and steers them toward the checkout.

"Fresh produce is what I miss the most," Nat says. "What I wouldn't give for a big green salad with tomatoes."

"Next summer we'll grow our own," Miles said.

His mother bites her lip and leans briefly against

him. "With any luck, we'll be home next summer," she says, "and the sun will shine again. We're gonna garden. We're gonna downsize. We're gonna totally change our lifestyle.""

"You, garden?" Miles asks. "Yeah, right."

"I'm serious," his mother says.

He drapes one arm briefly over her shoulder and gives her a hug. Then he places their groceries—potatoes, a couple of onions, a few cucumbers, four cans of corn, and a bag of white rice—on the conveyor belt. Which is dead, of course. Like everything, electricity is rationed; coal-burning power plants have been shut down altogether, which is not the worst thing in the world.

"Find everything you need?" the checkout clerk says cheerfully.

"I guess," Nat says with glance to Miles; he can barely keep from laughing as he slides the groceries forward.

"How are you folks today?" a voice booms. It's an overly friendly manager-type; he looks them up and down.

"Just great, eh?" Nat says. She has mastered the northern Minnesota speech pattern, with a dash of Canadian thrown in.

"Find everything you need?" he asks. It must be the

required cheerful question.

"Any news on fresh produce?" Nat asks. "When we might see some lettuce?"

His toothy smile slips a bit. "I get my information from the government, same as you," he says. "As our governor says, 'Stay put and stay calm.'"

"Just curious," Nat says.

"You folks have a nice day," he says.

Once outside, Miles looks over his shoulder at the hulking, big-box grocery store. "Stay put and trust the government—yeah, right," he says.

Natalie shrugs. "The government is not always the problem."

"If we had stayed put in the suburbs, we'd be really hungry by now—or maybe beaten up like that family down the street."

"You don't know that!" Nat says sharply.

"My point exactly," Miles says.

They stuff the groceries into his mother's backpack and head toward home—with one more stop to make.

Three miles west of town, Miles downshifts for an intersection and a ramshackle country store. Once a gas station, it's now a flea market, used car lot, used everything place called Old But Gold. Dusty cars, many almost new, sit in rows, along with a lineup of racy-looking, late-model snowmobiles. Behind them are lines of sawhorse tables filled with junk: old lamps, tools, saws. A couple of large, scruffy guys sit in chairs out front, in the sun.

"Be careful," Nat says.

"Hey, these are my peeps," Miles says. "Butch and his dad, Albert." He lowers his dusty bandana as he walks forward.

"Howdy, Miles," Albert says, and raises his chin once. His son, Butch, a younger but dustier version, nods as well. Miles has hung out here more than once; he likes to look over the old equipment and old tools. Talk to guys. Learn stuff that he's never heard about in regular school or in his alternative school packets.

"How's biz today?" Miles asks.

"Like tits on a boar," the old man says. "Meaning, none. What can I do you for?"

"My radiator is a little low," Miles says with a nod toward his motorbike.

"That so?" the old man says; he strokes his chin.

"Yep," Miles says. "You wouldn't have some antifreeze?"

"Antifreeze," the father says with the same emphasis.

He and Butch glance sideways at each other. "Might," the old man says.

"But it's pricier all the time," Butch adds.

"Like how much?" Miles asks.

"Today, twenty bucks a gallon," Butch replies.

"Ouch!" Miles says, then adds, "But what can you do?" He says it with a theatrical sigh—as if they're all in this together.

"Roll your bike up to the gate, and Butch will take it from there," the old man says.

Miles signals to his mother, who steps away from the Kawasaki. Miles rolls the motorbike forward, then hands it off to Butch, who unlocks a padlock on a heavy chain. "Wait outside," he says, never fully turning his back to Miles.

"Sure," Miles says cheerfully, and goes to hang out with Nat. They look over the snowmobiles. Behind the board fence there is clattering—then the clank of a nozzle on a gas tank rim.

"Nice day anyway," Butch's dad says, glancing up at the pale sky.

On the way home, Nat is on her high horse again. "Twenty bucks for one gallon of gas! That's highway robbery—literally."

"We're lucky we can get it at all," Miles says.

Suddenly, Miles stares intently ahead. Orange traffic cones line the highway, and two sheriff's cars grow from the haze. Their noses are toed in toward the centerline—a funnel-like traffic stop. Two big pickups are paused; an officer is looking at one driver's license while another is holding a short hose and a siphon. A third officer waves a dusty car with a Blue Star sticker past the checkpoint.

"What is this?" his mother calls over Miles's shoulder with alarm. "It's not one of those 'locals only' things?"

"No. We're fine. Just be cool," Miles says. He slows into first gear as he approaches the law enforcement cars. A deputy waves them forward into the neck of the funnel, all the while giving the motorbike a close look.

"Don't say anything!" Miles murmurs, and pulls over an instant before the deputy holds up his hand.

"Hey, officer," Miles says cheerfully.

"Howdy."

"Everything okay today?" Miles asks.

"No real problems. Just checking for off-road diesel."

They glance toward the guy standing beside his big Dodge pickup; he doesn't look happy. "No diesel fuel here," Miles says, and raps the little tank below the seat.

"You live nearby?" the deputy asks.

Miles feels his mother tense up. "Yeah. Just off County Road 7. We're makin' our weekly grocery run."

"No lettuce again!" Nat says in a whiny voice.

The deputy gives them one more look up and down; his gaze ends up on the Kawasaki. "Be careful on that thing. The dust on the highway gets greasy."

"Will do," Miles says, and accelerates away.

After a block he feels his mother turn to look behind, then back to the front. "Why did you stop?" she hisses.

"He was going to wave us in," Miles calls back to her, "so I wanted to make the first move. It's like in poker: Whoever makes the first big move controls the game."

"My son, the poker player," Nat mutters.

Miles laughs and speeds along.

"And what did he mean by 'off-road' diesel?" his mother asks.

"It's fuel that farmers get at a big discount for their tractors," Miles replies. "Same fuel that any truck or car with a diesel motor can use, except that it has a red dye in it."

"So they were taking samples from those pickups and checking the color?"

Miles nods. "And if it comes up red, you got

some explaining to do."

"How do you know all this stuff?" she asks as they motor along.

Miles shrugs. "It's sort of a guy thing."

"Well, enough with the guy stuff. Just get me home," she says, and holds him tighter from behind.

CHAPTER ELEVEN

SARAH

EVERY WEEKEND, IT'S HER TURN to lug buckets of water from the outside hand pump back to the cabin. She has slept in—it's Saturday—but now has to work. "I think it's Miles's turn," she says to her father.

"No, honey. Saturday means it's your turn," her father says.

Clanging the bucket loudly against the doorframe, Sarah heads outside to the well. Emily immediately starts to bounce around her pen and clack her front hooves high up on the boards.

"I can't play," Sarah mutters. "Not now." During her third trip with a full bucket, she looks up. Miles and her mother *putta-put* through the woods. Miles, a maniac for saving gas, kills the engine so that he coasts down the hill, dust flying, Nat hanging on tightly behind him.

"Groceries. Mail call!" Miles shouts. He dismounts and slaps dust from his pants.

"How'd it go?" Artie asks.

Nat slips off her backpack and glances at Miles—who shrugs and grins. "Just your basic trip to the grocery store."

Nat lets out a long breath.

Art narrows his eyes. "Did something happen?" he asks quickly.

"Yeah, the volcanoes," Miles says.

"Here," Nat adds, handing the heavy backpack to Sarah. "Put away the groceries. I really need to relax."

"I have to do everything around here!" Sarah groans.

For Miles and her parents, Saturday and Sunday are no different from any other day. For Sarah, the weekend feels like a week. Time slows down. The cabin gets smaller and smaller, especially after sundown.

That evening her mother reads and her father lightly

but continually *tap-tap*s his fingers as he reads music charts and listens to his headphones. Miles pores over Mr. Kurz's logbooks. "Look, Sarah—he even kept track of how much per month he spent on tobacco." Miles is so engrossed in the narrow ledgers that he actually calls her by her real name.

"How interesting," she says sarcastically. She glances briefly over Miles's shoulder at the cramped handwriting, the tidy columns of numbers.

"He smoked more in the winter," Miles observes, "like twice as much."

"Who wouldn't?" Sarah mumbles, glancing around the cabin.

"We'll all be smoking by spring," Nat says. It's a joke, but no one laughs.

"'December 1949; one Christmas card, ten cents,'" Miles reads.

"One Christmas card," Artie says, looking over. "That's sad." He actually listens sometimes.

"Wonder who he sent it to," Nat says.

"Probably to himself," Sarah says.

Miles looks up, suddenly angry. "What do you know about him? You never even met him."

After supper, as a gesture to Miles, she picks up one of Mr. Kurz's account books and looks through it. "What's 'logwood dye'?" she asks.

"For trapping," Miles says, his eyes lighting up. "He boiled his traps in water, paraffin, and this kind of black dye, which takes away the human scent and lubricates the iron—plus prevents it from rusting." As he talks, his eyes go ever so slightly crossed—not crossed really, but sort of blank: He's pulling stuff back from Mr. Kurz. She remembers that look from back home when, as kids, they played Memory, a matching game that Miles always won. His brain is the tiniest bit scary.

"Trapping, ick," she says.

"By the way," Miles announces to everyone, "we all need to learn how to shoot."

There is a moment of dead air.

"Why?" Nat says.

Miles rolls his eyes. "To protect ourselves. If Dad and I are off somewhere, it would be nice to know that you and Sarah could handle a gun."

"Me? Shoot a gun?" Nat says. "That will be the day."

"I could try," Sarah says suddenly. "I mean, at least learn how. Get my northern-girl thing on."

That night Sarah arranges her sleeping bag in her corner of the new bedroom—which smells strongly of pine. Miles has drawn a line down the middle of the floor: her side, his side. She decorates her "room" with her favorite stuffed animal (a purple-and-black zebra), a picture of her and her friends from fifth grade crammed into a photo booth at the state fair, along with stuff she has collected near the cabin: a weathered pine knot that looks like a little galaxy; several smooth stones from the river; and an open, empty clamshell: her mother-of-pearl butterfly. By candlelight she starts to read her favorite vampire novel, but all she can think about is Ray. She stares at the little yellow flame of the candle, then checks her watch. Only about thirty-six hours until the weekend is over.

In the morning, she wakes up before Miles—before everybody. No surprise there; she fell asleep around nine P.M. As Miles breathes heavily in his bag, she slips on her clothes and heads to the outhouse. The air is chilly but clear; the eastern sky is purple and pink.

On the path to the outhouse, she stops. To the far side, by their "burner barrel"—a rusty old fifty-gallon drum in which Miles burns trash—is movement: It's the gimpy dog, pawing through garbage. He has tipped over the whole barrel.

Her first instinct is to shout "Shoo!" or "Go away!" But for some reason she doesn't. She watches. The dog is so intent on finding something to eat that he doesn't see or hear her. He's totally ugly: a torn ear, long ago healed, split into two flaps; a gray muzzle; and that crooked and dangly right rear leg.

Suddenly he turns and sees her; he hunches down as if to run. But he has also found a scrap of fish skin that hangs from the side of his mouth like a skinny tongue.

Sarah slowly squats down. His yellow eyes follow her. Still watching her, he gulps down the fish skin, then resumes his pawing.

"You're making a mess," Sarah says softly.

His nose continues to nudge through the scattered garbage.

"What's your name?"

As she raises up slightly, he growls, but it's not a scary growl. Sarah really has to pee, so she stands, keeping her posture low, and eases past. Her movements, slow and nonthreatening, seem to work. He doesn't run.

When she returns, he's gone. With an old rake, she

comes back to clean up the mess and set the barrel upright. As she works, she raises her head and gradually stops moving; slowly she pivots her face to look behind her, into the brush. The old dog, almost perfectly camouflaged, watches her. Once her eyes stop on his, he melts backward into the brush.

"Brush," Sarah says. "That's your name."

MILES

OCTOBER ROLLS ALONG LIKE SUMMER, warm and hazy and dry. Miles skims the front page. *The unnaturally warm weather is a result of the earth's heat trapped under the worldwide dome of dust, including sulfurous compounds from the volcanoes, their gas miles up in the air, that react with oxygen and water to form aerosols that continue to linger worldwide.*

"In other words, a yellow freaking mist with a hang time of two to three years," Miles mutters, and tosses aside the newspaper. "Who writes that stuff?"

"Did you say something?" Artie asks, popping out one earbud.

"No," Miles says, and heads outside the cabin. He gets his nature facts not from scientists or the news but from keeping his eyes open. That, and from Mr. Kurz's notes on the local birds and critters. Robins, finches, wrens—should have gone south a month ago, but they're still here chirping and fluttering as they feed on bugs and seeds. Nature is one tough mother, but she takes care of the survivors. In the woods around the cabin male ruffed grouse, or partridge, are calling. *Boom . . . boom . . . boom . . . boom-boom . . . boom-boom-boom—boomaboomabooma!* go their wings as they stand on logs and beat their wings in the air. The sound is like someone trying over and over to start an old tractor. But really it's the sound of life moving forward despite the volcanoes.

Artie comes out of the cabin wearing his work gloves. "Let's do our thing," he calls to Miles.

Gathering firewood is what Miles and his father do best: saw up dead trees—most of them blowdown—then cut off the limbs with a short axe (Artie is the axe man) and later dice the logs into blocks with a vintage but very sharp two-man crosscut saw. Artie on one end, Miles on the other. Back-and-forth strokes, not fast, not slow, but with a steady rhythm. A beat, almost. Power chainsaws are cheap—there are plenty of used ones at Old But Gold—but they are also stinky, dangerous, and loud. A chainsaw engine can be heard for miles.

They knock out one long pine tree, then take a break to catch their breaths.

"Watch this," Artie says to Miles.

Miles straightens up to see.

With the short trimming axe in one hand, his father steps off five paces from a big standing dead tree. Like a tennis player bobbing backward for a serve, he swings the axe over his head—and launches it in a one-armed throw. The shiny axehead whips its handle end over end in the air—until the whole thing clanks against the tree trunk and falls to the ground.

"Dang," his father says. "I stuck two in a row yesterday."

After the firewood is cut, Miles heads over to work on the little winter stall for Emily. Sarah has been helping him with that on weekends and after school; when it comes to Emily or that stray dog, she's always right there. He has hardly pounded two nails when she shows up and stands there, watching. Micromanaging.

"How's Emily going to stay warm outside in winter?" Sarah asks.

"Her own body heat," Miles says. "That's why her shed has to be small."

"She'll freeze to death!"

"We'll put down a thick layer of sawdust, then fill it up with leaves. She'll be totally cozy."

"She'd better be," Sarah grumbles.

"Well she ain't sleeping in the cabin," Miles replies, banging home another nail.

"She's *not* sleeping in the cabin," Sarah says.

"That's what I said," Miles answers.

A flock of about a dozen ducks flies over low. They are mallards—green-headed males and dusky brown females. The lead duck cups the white undersides of its wings for a touchdown upriver. They've been coming and going, morning and night, in the same landing pattern for the last few days. Miles cocks his head. "I'm going hunting," he says suddenly, and hands his hammer to Sarah.

"We have to finish this!"

"Keep nailing boards," Miles says. "I won't be gone long." He takes his shotgun and heads along the riverbank.

The mallards are just upstream, out of sight in thin yellow reeds; they chuckle and quack and bob. Staying low, Miles creeps closer until he is within shotgun range. A big greenhead male floats into the open; Miles raises his gun. *Never shoot more than once during a day. One shot, and nobody knows for sure where it came from. It's the second shot that tells them where you are.* His finger tightens on the trigger, but a brownish female mallard paddles into view, blocking his shot. A mother duck. Three smaller ducks paddle behind her—a little family—and Miles can't bring himself to pull the trigger. She flutters through the reeds, and immediately the little ducklings swim behind her, pecking at the water. Miles squints. Leans forward to look closer. The duck family is eating wild rice. He should have remembered this—the wild rice— from Mr. Kurz's stories.

He stands up suddenly—the mallards quack loudly and flare straight up from the water—but he doesn't shoot. Instead, he heads quickly back to the cabin.

Sarah spots him as he emerges from the brush. "Did you get anything? I didn't hear you shoot."

"Didn't want to shoot. Got something better. Put down the hammer; we're going wild ricing!"

In the battered, camouflage-painted canoe (another score from Old But Gold), he and Sarah paddle upstream. His shotgun lies in the bottom of the boat, along with two skinny sticks. *Use wooden sticks: one to bend the rice plants over your canoe, the other to knock the heads off. That's what your flail stick is for. Bend and flail, bend and flail. If the rice beds are good, you can make a hundred dollars a day. Me, I only riced for what I needed to eat. One sack of raw, green rice was plenty. Then you have to clean it and dry it—parch it slow over a wood fire in a big iron kettle, one that's heavy enough so the rice won't burn. Most people are not good at parching. They want to cure it fast, but it takes time. . . .*

"I don't know what I'm doing," Sarah says.

"Just paddle," Miles says to her.

"I knew there was a reason you put me in the back." She groans.

"The stern," Miles says. "I'm in the bow."

"Where do I paddle?"

"Right through there," Miles says, pointing to the rice bed. The stalks tower head-high alongside the canoe—and grains of rice fall at first touch.

"Slower!" Miles calls back to Sarah. Clumsily he works the two sticks. Lots of rice falls into the water, but more and more of the little heads fall into the canoe. Gradually Miles finds the right rhythm and touch.

"Ick—the grains have little green worms!" Sarah says.

"More protein," Miles says.

"They're sharp, too," she says of the little rice spears; she tries to brush them off, but they stick to her jeans.

"We're lucky there's any rice left," Miles says. "Keep going."

They work back and forth through the river bend for an hour, until the bottom of the canoe is furry and thick: a shaggy carpet of raw, green rice.

"Can we go home now?" Sarah whines.

"Okay, okay," Miles says. As they leave, a flock of mallards wheels high overhead, then banks to make a tight circle above the rice bed. "Thanks," Miles murmurs.

"You're welcome," Sarah says, clanking her paddle.

He doesn't explain.

As they paddle downstream, there is brown motion in the undergrowth. "There's that dog!" Miles says suddenly. On the shore, he lurks from tree to tree, following them home.

"Brush!" Sarah calls. "Hey, Brush!"

"Don't encourage him! And never feed him," Miles says. "That's why he hangs around—he knows we have food."

"Maybe he used to live here," Sarah said. "Maybe he was Mr. Kurz's dog."

Miles spits sideways into the water and keeps paddling. "He would have to be, like, a hundred dog years old. He's just a stray dog who's not going to make it through the winter."

"He could live with us and be our watchdog," Sarah says.

"He only has three good legs. Great watchdog."

"What will happen to him?"

"Don't ask me," Miles says as they head on a straight course downriver.

SARAH

AT SCHOOL SHE STAYS INVISIBLE except on the tennis court. The coach lets her play—red-shirt status, which means she's "unofficially" on the team—and today she is panting and sweaty after beating Carolyn 6–3 and 6–1. As she tilts up her water bottle, Ray approaches the chain-link fence. She pretends not to notice him until the last second.

"Hey," he says.

"Oh—hi, Ray."

They pause to watch the green tennis balls fly back and forth.

"Haven't see you around much lately," Ray says.

"You either."

They are silent. Then Ray says, "Remember that football game?"

"Yes."

"You said you'd talk to me in school."

"I do talk to you!" Sarah says, turning.

"But not talk-talk. You know, like 'quality time.'"

Sarah giggles. "It's not like we're going steady."

Ray's face reddens slightly. "You know what I mean."

She is silent. "Sort of."

They watch Mackenzie, who is also watching them—and because of it misses the ball.

"Lucky shot," Mackenzie snaps, and slams a serve straight at Rachel, who ducks. To the side is Mackenzie's dad; he often comes to watch practice.

"Hey, Sarah, want to step in?" Rachel calls. She is limping slightly.

Sarah glances at the coach.

"Why not?" the coach says.

On the court, Sarah bounces the ball twice, then lobs a nice serve to Mackenzie's forehand. Slowly they volley back and forth; and from the rhythm, and the sunlight on the clean and tidy court, her mind starts to drift. Back home. Home-home to the suburbs, where the biggest problem she had was going over her cell phone minutes. Back then, she and her mother had their I've-had-a-really-really-bad-day signal: holding two rackets. It required the other—no questions asked—to stop everything and come hit tennis balls.

Only now does Sarah understand how cool that was—how she and her mother didn't have to say anything; they would just volley back and forth. She and her mother with their tennis rackets and the furry green balls that they hammered back and forth until one of them called "Enough!" One time they played until they could barely walk back to the house and were laughing and bumping into each other as they scarfed down leftovers and then just lay on the soft carpet by the big fireplace. They left the television off and for two hours talked about things. About Sarah's friends. About her mother's clients. About life. Things like that didn't happen too often back then. But Sarah now had to admit one thing: If she had to live in a small cabin with someone's mother, hers wasn't all that bad.

"Hey!" Mackenzie calls as Sarah's hard serve skips past her.

"Come on, Mac!" her father calls. "Pay attention out there!"

"Sorry!" Sarah says; she sneaks a glance toward Mackenzie's father, who stands, watching. She has to get a grip, remember where she is. Who she is. But Ray is watching; she goes after Mackenzie harder: hitting the corners, dropping soft ones with reverse spin just over the net.

"You really can play!" Mackenzie calls; there is accusation in her voice.

Sarah answers with her hardest serve of the afternoon—directly at Mackenzie. The ball ricochets once and catches her in the belly.

"Ooomph!" Mackenzie grunts as the ball dribbles off. She clatters her racket into the corner, where it bangs off the fence, and then she stomps off the court.

"Nice strokes, Sarah," says the coach. "I knew you were a player."

Behind the fence, Mackenzie's dad folds his arms across his chest.

Mackenzie will not speak to Sarah for the rest of practice and leaves with her father without even looking at Sarah.

The next morning in school she is smiley again.

"Sorry I was such a bitch," she says.

"Hey, no problem. I was playing way over my head."

"It's just my competitive nature," Mackenzie says. "Sometimes it comes out wrong."

Sarah shrugs. "I know what you mean. And really, it's no big deal. I've forgotten about it."

"Anyway, I was thinking," Mackenzie says, "you and I could be doubles partners. We'd kick butt!"

"That might be cool," Sarah says, which is a lie.

"So let's practice late tonight," Mackenzie says. "My dad said he could drive you home."

Sarah frowns as if she'd like to stay and practice but can't. "I need to be home right after practice. We have to . . . take our boat in. For the winter. All-hands-on-deck sort of thing."

"I could help," Mackenzie says. "We could stay over at your house tonight!"

"Ah, it's kind of a mess right now. We're doing some remodeling. But when that's done, sure."

Mackenzie shrugs. "Okay. So how about a sleepover tomorrow tonight at my house? That will give us extra practice time."

Sarah thinks of the hot shower, the bathtub, toilets with actual running water. "Okay."

At the cabin that night during supper—fresh northern pike from the river and newly parched wild rice— she mentions the upcoming sleepover.

"Fine, I guess," Nat says to Artie.

"Sure," Artie says, sorting out a tiny Y-bone from his fish.

Miles is silent, then mutters something under his breath.

"What?" Sarah asks him.

He shrugs. "Pretty soon you'll be staying in town all the time."

"It's just a one-night sleepover," she says.

"You're gonna dump us for hot running water and toilets," Miles says.

"Hot water and soap is a good thing," Nat says. They all look at Miles.

"And, by the way, what are you pounding on all the time over by the sawmill?" Sarah asks.

"Nothing," Miles says quickly.

On Thursday night, after a long practice and a deliciously long hot shower at Mackenzie's house, it's time for dinner with the Phelps family. Jane is cheerful as always, but Mackenzie's father is quieter than normal. Mitzy, who has her own chair and cushion, peeks up above the tabletop; her little dark eyes follow the food bowls as they are passed. Every once in a while Jane slips Mitzy a tiny bite of food.

"So how are things at home?" Bill asks Sarah.

"Fine, thanks," she says quickly. "We finally got our boat in. My parents are busy getting the place ready for winter, that sort of thing," she says.

He narrows his eyes. "Ready for winter?"

"It needs . . . some winterizing. It's actually our summer place—The Cottage, we call it."

"I see," Bill says as he passes the casserole dish to his wife.

"We *must* meet your parents, soon!" Mackenzie's mom says, and touches Sarah's arm.

"For sure," Sarah says, matching her with cheeriness. "But they love being on the river so much that it's hard to get them away from there. I mean, it's so pretty where we live."

Bill Phelps makes a throat noise, and the dinner continues with a focus on Mackenzie's tennis career. Once or twice Sarah is certain that Mackenzie's dad is staring at her.

After dinner, she and Mackenzie do the dishes while Jane takes Mitzy for a walk. Mr. Phelps watches television, though sometimes he watches Mackenzie and Sarah—Sarah can feel his gaze.

Suddenly Mackenzie's cell phone plays. She opens it. "It's Django!" she mouths to Sarah, and disappears up the stairs.

Then it's just Sarah in the kitchen. She rattles the dishes loudly as she works.

Bill gets up and comes into the kitchen behind her.

"Hi," Sarah says stupidly.

He glances around, then back to her. "I want you to know that I know."

"Excuse me?"

"I know that you don't have a home on the Mississippi River," he adds, keeping his voice low. "I've checked at the courthouse and in the plat maps, and there's no record of you."

"It . . . we inherited the cottage from my grandmother," Sarah says quickly. "It's probably still in her name."

"Don't lie. You're only getting yourself in deeper," he says. "I've also made some calls to the Hubbard County courthouse. Nobody down there has ever heard of your family."

Sarah swallows. She's rinsing silverware and just happens to have a butter knife in her hand.

"Which means just one thing," Bill continues, keeping his voice down. He glances around. "You and your family are Travelers."

"What?!" Sarah exclaims. She manufactures a laugh, but it comes out fake and strangled.

"So let me give it to you straight," Bill says, leaning closer. He has her cornered in the kitchen. She can smell his breath; it's sour and grapy with wine. "I suggest that you just disappear. From this community. From this school. You have no future here. If you don't, I'll blow the whistle on you; and the sheriff will find you— wherever you and your family are squatting."

A door bangs.

"Mitzy saw a squirrel!" Jane says from the hallway. "And she barked at it—as if she's any danger to a squirrel!"

Bill Phelps pivots to pick up a dirty plate and pretends to be rinsing it.

"Hey, you two don't have to do the dishes!" Jane says cheerfully as she comes into the kitchen.

"No problem," Sarah says, slipping the knife into the dishwasher.

"Just trying to get to know Sarah a little better," Bill says.

"That's so sweet of you," his wife says, and gives him a quick kiss. "Now, you go read your newspaper, and I'll help Sarah finish up."

Luckily, the dishes are nearly all put into the dishwasher. "I guess I'll head up and see if Mackenzie's off the phone," Sarah says.

Once out of sight up the carpeted stairs, she pauses to grip the railing and get her breath. Her heart is slamming inside her chest like an insane clock. Mackenzie laughs once behind her bedroom wall. Sarah heads for the hall bathroom, where she locks the door. She sits down on the closed toilet seat and looks around: the shiny bathtub, the faucets, the gleaming chrome, the fluffy rugs on the tile floor, the lineup of shampoo and conditioners and colored body washes. The whole room tilts as if she might faint—but she keeps taking deep breaths until her heartbeat slows.

"Hey," Mackenzie says when Sarah enters the room.

Sarah musters a smile.

Mackenzie cocks her head. "Are you all right? Your face is, like, white."

"Sure," Sarah says. "I think I ate too much. Or something."

In the morning she wakes up exhausted. Mackenzie's

bedroom is too hot, the bed is too soft, and Mitzy kept nuzzling around all night on top of the covers.

"Shower?" Mackenzie mumbles.

"No rush. You go first," Sarah says.

As water hisses behind the bathroom door, Sarah looks around the bedroom. It's totally girly in whites and pinks, with wall posters of boy bands. It feels like a room from a movie set or a museum. A diorama dedicated to showing how teenage American girls once lived. She has a vision of shabby people from the future passing through this very bedroom on a guided tour; they murmur and point at things in disbelief. The marked path on the white carpet is worn down to its mesh by rough sandals and boots. Mackenzie's big bed is roped off. The closet and the chest of drawers are open for ease of viewing. All the clothes. The endless pairs of shoes. The tour ends at the bright bathroom, with its soaps and bottles of shampoo and conditioner, its long, fluffy towels. In the line of gawkers are the little girls from the Travelers' minivan. They are now teenagers but even prettier with their cornrow hair—and when the museum guide is not looking, they reach across to touch the soft, stuffed animals on the bed. Examine the tubes of lipstick and eyeliner in the bathroom. With a guilty look over their shoulders, they quickly replace things exactly as they were and shuffle forward. The line is moving again—it's a busy day at the Museum of the American Teenage Girl.

After Mackenzie finishes her shower, the bathroom is humid, and Sarah locks the door and takes her turn. A long, slow shower with her eyes closed. Afterward, as she dries off, she looks about the bathroom. Its big mirrors. Its counters full of beauty products, perfumes, lotions. She rummages through a drawer of deodorants and soaps and nail polish. Takes—okay, steals—an unwrapped bar of lavender-scented soap. It's not like she's ever coming back to this house.

After her Thursday-night sleepover at Mackenzie's house and a long day at school on Friday, Sarah (and her stolen bar of lavender soap) comes home on the orange bus. Miles is waiting just out of sight in the woods, as usual.

"Ready for a fun-filled weekend?" he calls to her.

She stands unmoving as the bus rumbles away.

"What?" he says. "It was a joke."

She plods down the ditch, then past him.

"Bad day?" Miles asks.

"You don't want to know," she mumbles as they head down the forest path.

"That's why I don't go to regular school," Miles says behind her.

They soon arrive on the ridge above the cabin. She pauses to look down at the scene: the shack, the little wooden-walled add-on room she has to share with stinky Miles. Toward the woods the narrow, square outdoor toilet with its cold seat, poopy-stinky smell, and cobwebs on the ceiling. The sawmill, the junk pile—the little corral where Emily hops up and down when she sees Sarah.

"So how was school?" her mother calls from across the yard. She's reading manuscripts on the little front porch.

"It wasn't—it isn't," Sarah says. She drops her backpack on the porch with a thud, slumps onto the front steps, and begins to sob.

"Artie!" her mother calls, and soon her parents are on either side of her.

"What happened?" her father asks.

In a blubbery rush of words she tells them everything.

"Whoa, what a creep!" Miles mutters.

"It's tennis," Nat says.

"Huh?" Sarah says, looking up.

"He didn't want you to compete with Mackenzie," Nat adds.

"Obviously," Artie adds.

"We all agree," Miles says.

"So?" Sarah says. "It doesn't change anything; I can't go back to school." Her chest starts heaving again.

Miles and his parents look at one another.

"I'll go crazy here!" Sarah says to them, jerking her head toward the cabin's door.

"What's wrong with here?" Miles asks.

CHAPTER FOURTEEN

MILES

THE NEXT WEEK AS HALLOWEEN approaches, the weather turns suddenly colder—more proof that both the news and the weather reports can't be trusted. The motorbike ride to town is downright freezing, but Miles and his mom score a pumpkin. It's no bigger than a grapefruit and more yellow than orange, plus it has a flat side. Back home inside the toasty-warm cabin, the whole family gathers around to stare at it. No one says anything. Finally Sarah breaks the silence. "That's the world's saddest-looking pumpkin."

"Not a good year for pumpkins," Miles adds, warming

his hands by the woodstove. The temperature outside is thirty degrees, but it's eighty in the cabin thanks to Art, who has become Mr. Firewood.

"And you don't want to know what I paid for that thing!" Nat says.

"Why did you buy it, anyway?" Sarah asks. "It's not like we're going to get any trick-or-treaters out here."

"We need to keep our family traditions—celebrate things. Otherwise, what do we have?" Art says.

They all look at one another. Art talking about family togetherness is more than a little strange, but he has been different—more with the program—ever since Sarah's run-in with Mr. Phelps. It's as if the incident was some weird kind of wake-up call to fatherhood.

"Okay, then—let's carve our giant pumpkin!" Sarah says sarcastically.

"We should make a design first," Art says.

"I agree," Nat says.

Miles flashes on Birch Bay, when his grandparents were still alive and he was really small—when time was different, when a day was a week long.

"We each come up with a drawing," Art says. "Then we have a vote—and the winner gets to carve the pumpkin."

Miles and Sarah look at each other. Sarah rolls her eyes. "This is, like, fourth grade."

"Fourth grade was fun with you two," Art says.

"I've got paper and pencils," Nat says.

"And no rush, everybody," Miles says. "We have all night."

"No kidding," Sarah grumbles, but sets to work on her drawing; she's careful not to let Miles see it. The whole family sits around the table, hunched over their drawings, shielding their design from one another with one hand and drawing with the other.

"No peeking!" Sarah says to Miles.

"I wasn't!" he throws back.

Sarah has the winning design (they've all agreed not to vote for themselves). Using the flat side of the pumpkin as a forehead, she carefully carves out long ears and horizontal eyes to create a decent-looking goat face.

"Emily!" Miles says. "That's pretty good."

"Watch this," Sarah says. When she lights a little candle inside, Emily's bright, narrow eyes stare back.

Artie leans back. Looks around. "This must be what it was like," he says.

"What what was like?" Sarah asks.

"Families. Way back in the day."

No one says anything.

"I mean, before cell phones and internet and television and even telephones," he continues.

"You mean before electricity," Nat asks.

"Yeah," Miles says. "Not only off the grid—no grid."

"If you think about it," Artie says, "what was there to do?"

"Nothing!" Sarah says. She tries to be sarcastic, but it doesn't work.

"Exactly," Miles says. "You had to make stuff up. Like we're doing right now."

She gives him a dark look—as if he's a traitor for siding with a parent.

"Play games, sing songs," Art continues.

"Forget it! I'm not singing," Sarah says.

"Or do nothing at all," Nat says, and leans against Art.

Sarah rolls her eyes. Wood crackles in the stove, and in the small, warm cabin they sit and watch the flicker of the fire in the tiny glass window of the stove's door.

Much later that night Miles awakens. It's deep dark. There's a different scent—a thicker, cooler air. He listens: The woods outside the cabin are quieter than usual. No night sounds at all. No hooting owls, no night critters scampering across the roof. He steps quietly over Sarah and goes to the cabin door.

Snow! Giant, wet flakes falling like albino leaves. The ground is totally covered; the trees, too. Trick or treat from the weather gods. Back in the day, back in his old life as a kid, the first snow would have been a thrill. Now he is filled with dread. He breathes deeply, filling his lungs with the clean, wet air—several breaths of it—until he's calmer.

"Winter's coming," his father says behind him.

Miles jumps. "You scared the bejesus out of me."

"Sorry," his father says as he continues to stare at the falling snow.

"I hope we can do this," his father says.

"Do what?" Miles says, though he knows what his father means.

"Get through the winter. Go back home someday."

"'Back home' might not be there," Miles replies, turning sideways to his father.

His father looks straight at him.

They return their eyes to the window and are silent as they watch the falling snow.

At first light, Miles takes his gun and slips outside. In

the new snow, dog prints circle the burner barrel (Sarah has been feeding him). *New snow is an open book—if you know how to read it.* He heads up the ridge above the cabin, but the snow is unmarked except for a line of heart-shaped deer hooves unwinding like a necklace across the throat of the woods.

Walking quietly on the soft snow, he eases through the oak trees. Heel to toe. Slowly. As soundlessly as he can. Ahead, a moving shadow—a patch of brown: a deer among the tree trunks! He lifts his gun; a fawn pauses to look around. It's an easy shot, but he holds his fire: The weather is still not cold enough to keep the meat. The little deer bobs its head and flicks its stubby, brown-and-white tail—then picks up a scent (Miles) and bounds off. It's a deer he would never have seen without the white backdrop of snow.

Down by the river there are mink tracks along the shore. Fox tracks, too. A fox leaves a single-file track: Its two rear paws step exactly where the front paws have landed. Less energy expended—especially in snow—and fewer tracks left behind. In nature, everything makes sense.

He is about to head back to the cabin when he sees the old dog. At first he thinks he's dead—frozen in place—as he approaches him from behind, but his neck is erect. The old mutt with the tattered collar watches the cabin and yard. Miles steps on a branch, which cracks and flips forward. The motion, not the noise, startles the dog. He whirls toward Miles, and the hair on his back goes up like the dorsal fin on a shark. They have a long moment—two predators in full eye contact—then, scrambling, the dog runs, throwing snow from his claws. Despite his lame leg, he is incredibly fast. Once into the riverbank brush, he pauses to look back.

"Hey!" Miles says, and pitches a stick at him.

The dog does not flinch. He's either stupid or afraid of nothing.

CHAPTER FIFTEEN

SARAH

"WANT TO HELP ME WITH some firewood?" her father asks from the doorway to the bedroom.

Sarah shrugs. "I guess. It's not like I'm doing much." She puts down her vampire novel, which she has reread for the tenth time.

Outside, they haul and stack dead limbs that her father has cut and sawed by hand.

"Do you miss regular school?" her father asks.

She shrugs angrily.

"You probably met at least some nice kids there," he says, taking one end of a heavy limb; together, they swing it onto the pile.

"Sort of," she mumbles.

"Any boys?" her father teases.

"The main reason I liked school was for the toilets and hot running water," she says sharply.

Her father keeps working in silence.

"I mean," Sarah continues, "how are we going to, like, bathe when it's winter?"

"Bathe? I thought you'd never ask!" Miles says as he comes around the side of the sawmill. He's totally sweaty but as happy as a clam.

"In the river, I suppose," Sarah says. "Cut a hole in the ice. Jump in. Well, forget that."

"No, no, no," Miles says impatiently. He gestures to them, then calls for Nat. "I have a surprise for you!" he announces to his family.

Sarah brings up the rear as they follow him around the corner of the sawmill. Attached to one side of it is a lean-to eight feet square. Board walls. Wooden door. A small iron pipe poking through the roof.

"This thing you've been working on," Nat says, "what is it?"

"Step inside and you'll see," Miles says. He couldn't be more pleased. This whole environmental disaster has been just perfect for him, Sarah thinks.

Cautiously, Nat opens the door and goes in, followed by Artie and Sarah. There are four sturdy wooden benches, like bunk beds—one on each wall.

"I don't get it," Sarah asks. "We already made an extra bedroom."

"It's a sauna," Artie says. He smiles widely.

Miles beams from the doorway. "Exactly! That's how people bathed in the old days. Take a sauna, then take a roll in the snow."

"A roll in the snow?!" Sarah says.

"It would certainly get you clean," Nat says, looking directly at Miles.

Who of course misses her point.

"Do you guys like it?" he says enthusiastically.

"It's great," Artie says. "I thought you were building a storage shed or something."

Miles is so pleased he actually giggles.

"It's certainly . . . rustic," Nat says.

They all look at Sarah. "That's, like, a woodstove?" she asks, pointing.

"Exactly," Miles says, leaning down beside a small iron drum. "I recycled this little barrel. Cut a hole on top for a stovepipe, another one down low for air and to get sticks of wood in. It works great! When it's twenty below zero, we can have family sauna nights!"

They all look at one another.

"Will we . . . all fit?" Nat asks politely.

"Hey, we're in here now," Miles answers. He steps all the way in, then pulls shut the door behind him.

Instantly it's pitch-dark in there, except for a few pinholes and slivers of light. Miles swears. Sarah would laugh if she weren't so claustrophobic.

"Lights! Dammit—I forgot about lights!" Miles says.

"Candles would work," Artie offers.

"I have to get out of here!" Sarah says, stumbling against Miles as she escapes. The door clatters open; light spills back into the small, boxy sauna.

"What's wrong with her?" Miles says.

"Leave her be," she hears her father say.

At supper Miles can't stop talking about the sauna; Artie and Nat try to humor Sarah.

"Don't," she mutters to them. "My life is over, okay?"

They continue eating. The meal is river fish, rice, beans, and goat's milk. Emily is not giving much milk these days, but there's still a big glass to share. Sarah flashes on dinners back home-home: the giant kitchen with designer copper pots hanging above the stainless steel cooktop; the big dining-room table that they hardly ever used. They usually sat at the counter in a row, nobody really facing anyone else; or else they had "bowl dinners" so they could watch television while they ate. Here they bump knees. They can't avoid one another.

"I'm really sorry about school," Nat says again to Sarah.

Sarah shrugs. "I suppose I could do school online—but, oh, I forgot. We don't have internet because we don't have electricity," she says sarcastically.

"You could do alternative school with me!" Miles says.

"In my next life, maybe," Sarah mutters.

"Hey, the AEC is not that bad," Miles said. "There's some fairly cool teachers there."

"Forget it!" Sarah says, and stomps off to her—their—room. She lies there thinking about Ray: the dark wing of hair that kept falling over his right eye. His bony but square shoulders. His long fingers. How they always felt burning hot when he touched her arms or hands. Or, one time, her face.

The next morning, Miles disappears on his motorbike. When he comes back a couple of hours later, he is secretive but pumped about something.

At lunch he says to Sarah, "I got you something!"

"Huh?"

"An early Christmas present," Miles says. "Sit here. Close your eyes."

Sarah glances around the overly warm cabin. Art's veggie chili is cooking on the wood range.

"It's okay," her mother says.

"Hold out your hands!" Miles says.

She does. Then her fingers close around something smooth, heavy, and hard—like a piece of pipe or a round chair leg. She opens her eyes.

"Your very own shotgun!" Miles says. He's vibrating with excitement.

"Gee, thanks," Sarah says gingerly; she holds the gun away from her body.

"Careful!" Nat says.

"It's not loaded," Miles says with annoyance.

Just in case, Sarah keeps the muzzle end pointed to the ceiling. "Ah, it looks a lot like your old shotgun," she says. "The one that creepy Danny gave you."

"It is," Miles says. "I got another gun for myself: a twelve-gauge pump that holds five shells. But this .410 single shot will be a perfect starter gun for you."

"And just how did you get another gun?" Nat asks quickly.

"Get another gun? This is America!" Miles answers.

"Seriously," Nat says.

"Old But Gold," Miles says. "Anybody can buy a gun there.

"So start getting comfortable with it," he says to Sarah. "Shooting practice begins right after lunch. Then next week we can go deer hunting together."

Sarah glances again at her parents, who are of no help.

She takes her time eating. Miles wolfs down his veggie chili. "See you outside in five!" he says brightly.

After Miles is gone, her mother says, "You don't have to do this."

Sarah shrugs. "It's no big deal," she says, and carries her bowl to the washbasin.

Outside, Miles shows her how to hold the gun. How the safety works. She is wearing homemade earplugs made of toilet paper spitballs; his voice sounds far away.

"Ready to try it?" Miles has set up a rusty tin can as a target.

She nods.

Standing close behind her, Miles helps her fit the

stock against her shoulder. "Put your cheek right on the wood," he says.

She does.

"Okay!" Miles says.

She closes her eyes and very slowly squeezes the trigger, hard and harder. "Nothing's happening!" she says.

"The safety—click it to the off position," Miles says.

"I thought I did that," Sarah mutters.

"Must not have been off all the way," Miles says easily.

She takes another breath, looks down the barrel with both eyes open (as per Miles's instruction), and jerks the trigger.

Poom! The tin can goes flying.

"You hit it!" Miles says.

"Lucky shot," Sarah answers.

"No way," Miles says. "You're a natural. I can tell."

She shoots several more times and hits the can each time. Soon it's all torn and jagged.

"Right now you're shooting fine shot, "Miles explains. "Each shell has a bunch of little pellets in it. They spray out in a pattern about this big around." He holds his hands apart, thumbs curved, to make a hoop about the size of a basketball.

"Duh. So that's why I'm hitting the can every time."

"Sort of," Miles replies. "Now we need to practice shooting slugs."

"What's a slug?"

Miles holds up a .410 shell, which is about the size of his pinkie finger. "See this?"

She looks closer at the business end of the shell; a little rounded gray knuckle peeks out from the plastic sleeve.

"This is the slug," Miles explains. "It's one bullet. A single piece of lead. You wouldn't want to shoot at flying ducks with a slug because you'd never hit anything. A slug is more for deer and, well, self-protection."

"For shooting people, you mean?"

"If you had to," Miles says. He sets up another target: a bright aluminum pie plate. He instructs her to sight down the barrel by closing one eye this time. She aims, tries to hold steady, then fires at the plate. She misses twice but hits it the third time.

"Bingo!" Miles calls. He hurries over to retrieve the plate, then brings it back to Sarah.

There's a perfectly round hole in it about the size of a dime. On the back side, the aluminum is not peeled away or torn; the thin metal is just gone.

"Let me try it again," she says. Miles hands her another shell.

This time she imagines the pie plate as Bill Phelps's thick face. She rocks backward.

"Bull's-eye!" Miles calls, and slaps a one-armed hug on her. "You're a natural."

CHAPTER SIXTEEN

MILES

"LIKE I SAID, YOU DON'T have to shoot a deer," Miles whispers to her the first morning of hunting season. They are dressed in blaze orange and stand outside the cabin on new snow. "I just need you in the woods with your gun. If other hunters come around, they'll see that this area is taken."

"That we're armed, you mean." Her breath steams in the chilly air.

Miles smiles.

"So I just sit?" Sarah asks.

"Yes," Miles says impatiently. "I have a spot for you.

Sitting is mostly what hunting is about. Staying still and keeping your eyes open. Shooting is the least of it."

She slumps her shoulders.

"Look at things around you," Miles says with annoyance. "Nature is great."

After he gets Sarah situated in her little brush blind—with a pillow for her stump, a blanket for her legs, and a thermos of tea—he moves on down the trail. Before going out of sight, he turns to look back. She's motionless behind a half circle of branches. Her blaze-orange camo glows, but deer are color-blind. He waves once. She doesn't move.

Soon the woods belong to him. Walking as quietly as he can, he moves along the trail beneath some pine trees. *When you're deer hunting, stay out of trees. Only monkeys and squirrels climb trees. Every year, deer hunters fall out of tree stands and kill themselves. Used to be that a tree stand could be no more than six feet off the ground. That was the law. Six feet was plenty. If a hunter fell asleep and crashed down, at least he wouldn't break his neck. Then the game wardens said you could be twelve feet off the ground, then sixteen. Now, who knows how high? And why? You're only looking for trouble when you climb a tree or a ladder with a gun in your hands. Plus it's windier and colder the higher you go. What you want to do is use the land for your shooting angles. Get yourself on a side hill where you can see a trail below. Find a stump or a log to sit on, then build yourself a brush blind around it. Sit there. All day. If you can stick it out for a whole day, you'll get your chance at a deer. Most people can't sit that long. They get antsy. Got to get up and move. . . .*

Miles eases into his brush blind just before sunup. Like Sarah's, his is a black semicircle of dead branches about three feet high arranged around a stump, with an oak tree to lean his back against. He built it days ago but wanted to let it rest. Let it settle into the landscape. He sits on a gunnysack half full of sawdust, which drapes over the stump. The bag conforms to his butt and will give warmth to his legs. As he situates himself, a twig cracks beneath his boots; then a deer, unseen, crashes away through the gray-black woods. He swears silently; the deer must have been bedded down not far away. Quickly he gets settled. Stocking cap pulled low over his forehead, blanket over his legs, gun across his lap, and a lunch bag within reach—he's ready.

Gradually, the woods—the black trees, gray brush, and pale snow—forgets him and returns to its own business. A squirrel chatters, then rummages among fallen oak leaves. A partridge flaps from its night perch, goes silent on its glide downward, then flutters its wings through thick brush, a tattered baseball card on bicycle wheel spokes. A dark, wide-winged shadow glides by in absolute silence: an owl. A raven croaks and is answered by the chuckle of another. High overhead, duck wings whistle like a sewing machine on fast stitch. Gradually Miles's heartbeat slows. The oak tree becomes part of his back, his spine. His eyes are knotholes. There are occasional booming reports from the other hunters, but none close.

Deer season is when they come. State land brings in the hunters who don't own land themselves. That's as it should be. You ever see those signs: State Land—Keep Off? Well think about that. People are the state; but still, if you hunt on state land—or live there like I do—you got to stake out your territory. Guard it. No different from the old settler days. You got to get there first, make your claim, and let the other hunters know you're there. I used to make up a couple of dummies and put an orange vest and cap on each of them. That's all the other hunters need to see, that blaze orange behind some brush, and they keep moving.

He and Sarah. He hopes that the two of them are enough. His parents wanted no part of sitting around the woods in the cold and snow.

As he waits, first light climbs down the trees branch by branch. Oak leaves and then pine needles come into focus. The wall of the forest gradually opens like curtains on a stage. As the light grows, the deer trail lengthens, unwinding among the trees; its narrow path of scuffed snow, dirt, and oak leaves are like the trail of a snake slowly sliding forward.

At that moment the buck arrives. He has come silently along the trail toward Miles—then materialized all at once as if assembled from the brown brush and black tree limbs. Smooth oak branches for legs. Barrel of a fallen log for its heavy neck and chest. Antlers curving up like old wild grapevines.

Miles clenches his gun under the lap blanket.

The buck pauses to listen, then keeps coming.

Miles eases off the safety, making sure it does not click, then slides his lap blanket to the side.

If a deer sees you first, it's already too late. Best just to stay still and wait for the next one. But if you see him first, he's yours. . . .

Suddenly the buck halts and bobs his head. He whistles—a sharp sucking in of air—to fix the strange scent. His tail erects and flickers white. He looks not at the brush blind but at the woods beside and beyond: Something is not right.

Miles throws his gun to his shoulder, and in the same motion the giant buck throws himself backward in a tangle of white flag, pale belly, black antlers, and oak-leaf-brown flanks. *Crash! crash! crash!* He's gone without a shot.

Damn! Miles lets out a breath. His heartbeat roars in his ears. He lowers the gun. Presses the safety.

He is shaky—glad to be sitting down and not in a tree—but he feels like a fool. What did he do wrong? The breeze was in his favor. He didn't move. He was in the right spot at the right time. The woods around him are silent. But they are aware of him now. Listening. Watching Miles, the stupid human who pretends he is a tree stump.

And he really has to pee.

Leaving his gun behind, he takes a short walk behind the blind. His bladder is full enough to write his name in snow—first and last, in cursive—but he concentrates on making the smallest steaming hole possible. He still feels shaky. In the middle of things, he looks up suddenly. The old dog is watching, lying thirty yards deep in the woods. The dog spooked the buck!

He lowers his eyes as if he has not seen the dog and finishes peeing. He zips up and kicks snow over his mark. Casually, as if in no hurry, he walks back to his brush blind. Out of sight behind the tree, he eases up his gun, clicks off the safety, then wheels around.

But the dog is not where he was.

He is not anywhere.

To make sure he was not seeing things, he walks deeper into the woods, tracking left and right until he spots a matted, melted spot in the snow. A dog bed of oak leaves. He swears, kicks at the wet oak leaves, then returns to his brush blind. Still steamed, he plops down and leans the gun against the tree. As if any deer will come now. He fights off the urge to go home. . . .

Not many people can last a whole day on a deer stand. If you can do it, you'll get your chance.

"I had my chance," he mutters. He pours a cup of lukewarm coffee and eats half of a cold fried-egg sandwich. After his snack, he settles back against the tree. Soon the forest slowly tips, rights itself, then tilts sideways again. His eyelids weigh a pound each. They droop and sag. He gives in to a nap—just a short one. . . .

He jerks awake with drool on his chin. The light is higher. Two chickadees flutter and peck close by. One suddenly lands on top of his stocking cap, walks across it, and gives him an upside-down look. He blinks, and the little bird darts away to the next tree, where it continues to feed. He wipes his chin and gathers his gun closer. *Bucks move in the middle of day, especially if they've been up all night horning around after does. They bed down at sunup, sleep a few hours, then start sniffing around again. When they're in full rut, they can't stop moving. . . .*

But through midday nothing stirs except gray squirrels and a small flock of Canada geese that comes over on its way to the river and the rice bed. He should be hunting them instead of deer.

Along about three P.M., the pale sunlight takes a slow step backward. The trees straighten. Listen. Among them and the leaves and the trail there is an expectancy. A feeling that something is going to happen. Miles's heartbeat kicks up a notch. He squeezes his gunstock, touches the safety, rests his finger near the trigger. Turning his head ever so slowly, he makes sure the dog is nowhere around, then focuses again on the trail.

By four P.M. the light turns gray and grayer. As the depth of field shortens, pine needles and the fine spear ends of brush fur, fuzz, turn indistinct. His heartbeat is running fast and steadily now, like river water channeled around a narrow bend. Something is going to happen.

Then, as if he has called him up from the forest, a little buck appears. Barely half the size of the big one, this deer is a "spike": two small, irregular antlers poke up in front of his big ears. The deer stops to paw for acorns, finds none, then continues closer, oblivious to the brush blind. To Miles's unsteady gun barrel, swaying as if he's suddenly on board a ship.

"Buck fever"—every hunter has it at some point. Men do crazy things—jack the shell out of the chamber, shoot into the ground—and swear they were aiming dead on. They can't figure out how they missed, but the real reason is buck fever.

Miles sucks in a deep breath, tries to hold steady, and fires. The shotgun rocks him, but he hears no report, no sound. The little buck wheels sideways and runs.

There is a blood trail on the snow, scarlet drips that turn to blotches, then to sprays of crimson. Blood on small aspen trees where the deer has ping-ponged against them—and then ahead, lying on the snow, the brown length of the deer himself. A wide-open eye with long and delicate lashes stares blankly at the sky.

To dress a deer, you start at his hind end. First roll him onto his back—and make sure his butt is pointing downhill. He'll drain out better that way. Work your knife around his bunghole, and be sure not to cut into his bladder. The goal is to keep the meat as clean as possible. After you've cut around his business end, you're ready to empty out the stomach. Make a small slit at the base of his belly, then put two fingers in there to hold it open. With the other hand, put your knife, blade up, between your fingers. Then move both hands upward, cutting only the skin. You want to keep the gut sack whole. Once you've cut all the way up the vee of the rib cage, you've got to reach in all the way to your elbows and cut those membranes that hold the gut sack in place. If you do it right, the whole thing will come loose in one big bag.

Kneeling, breathing hard, his arms elbow deep in hot blood, Miles works by feel. The steamy scent is like one of his mother's herbal teas, only stronger. Ranker. His stomach clenches as if he might throw up; but suddenly the jiggly sack is free inside the cavity. With both hands, he rolls it out like a big blubbery basketball.

Be sure to save the liver, and the heart, too. They're good eating. Cut 'em in thin slices and fry them up with onions.

"I don't think so," Miles murmurs. He goes to the front of the deer and pulls it forward by its antlers, away from the mess. The gobs of blood behind are already clotting into red, quivery jelly. Taking up his knife again, he closes his eyes and feels around farther up inside the chest for the heart and lungs, which must be removed.

The lungs are pink and foamy, the heart harder to find. Working by touch, he finally cuts it free. Lifts it out. It fits exactly in the palm of his hand. His shotgun slug has shredded the bottom lobe of the heart. A perfect shot.

The air is colder now, and with snow he scrubs blood from his forearms and wrists and hands. He washes with handfuls of snow. It melts away pink and watery, and the real color of his skin returns. He stuffs handfuls of snow inside the deer to clean it, too. The cradle of the ribs appears, pale boned, fresh, clean. As he works, a crow drifts over and caws to another. A raven squawks not far away, and in the brush, like a ghost, the old dog appears. Miles reaches for his gun, then stops himself. He needs to stay focused on his deer and get it back to the cabin before dark.

Removing his belt, he loops it around the little buck's neck and drags him away from the gut pile. The deer is surprisingly light—his brown hair slides easily on the snow—but then again, Miles is full of adrenaline. With every yard he moves away from the kill site, the old brown dog eases a yard closer. Miles stops; the dog stops.

After he has dragged the deer about a hundred feet,

the old dog is ten feet from the gut pile. Suddenly he lunges forward and gulps up a chunk of fat. Miles has plenty of time to lift his gun and get rid of the dog once and for all, but he doesn't. The old dog feels Miles's gaze, crouches lower for a moment, then snatches the deer's heart and runs.

CHAPTER SEVENTEEN

SARAH

BY NINE A.M. SHE'S COLD and totally bored—until two hunters appear on the trail heading toward her. They wear camo-pattern blaze orange and carry rifles with black telescopic sights. Both have dark, short beards. Taking a breath, she slowly stands up in her brush blind. She moves the gun into the open where the men can see it.

The other hunters pull up; they confer briefly, then turn around and slowly disappear back into the trees. She sits down; her heart goes *whumpa-whumpa* in her chest.

By midday the shooting has almost stopped, and

she heads back to the cabin for lunch and to warm up. Miles does not come in with her; he has packed his lunch.

"Did you see anything?" Nat asks.

"Some other hunters," Sarah says, "but they turned around when they saw me."

"That was Miles's plan," Nat says, sounding pleased.

"More like that old man Kurz's plan," Sarah says. She's cold and crabby. "How do you think Miles knows so much about the outdoors? It's not like he learned it in Minneapolis."

After lunch, she heads back to the woods. The shotgun on her shoulder feels lighter now, almost as if it's part of her body. It's kind of cool carrying a gun, and she makes a couple of sudden moves—draws down on an imaginary bad guy. *Boom.* And another bad guy behind her—*boom.* Mackenzie's dad—*boom!*

In her blind she's not sleepy now. At two o'clock a fat partridge glides into an aspen tree not far away—lands on a branch with a flutter of wing beats. For long moments it looks around, then starts to peck on the fine bud ends of another branch. She raises her gun and takes aim but cannot pull the trigger. And anyway, she's shooting a slug. As the afternoon drags on, she spends a lot of it thinking about Ray. Trying to remember every detail about him. His eyes. His teeth. His laughing mouth. The drawing pencil—a special kind with wide lead—that's always behind the raven's wing of hair over his ear.

Poom! A shot startles her. It comes from Miles's direction. She swivels her head to pinpoint the location, but a second shot doesn't come; she can't be sure it was him. She checks her watch and settles back onto her stump.

Thirty minutes later blaze orange appears among the trees.

Miles waves excitedly. "I got one!" he calls.

She gives a small wave in return. "Great."

He hurries up to her. "Want to see it?"

"Do I have to?"

"If you want to see your dog," Miles replies.

"Is he all right?" she asks quickly. Brush has been missing all day—she's sure it's because of the muffled gunshots across the countryside.

"Yes," Miles says. "Come on."

In the snow, more of which is falling, she trudges behind Miles.

"So there I was, totally hidden in my blind," he begins. Leading the way through the woods, he narrates the entire hunt like a documentary film in need of serious editing—including some parts she doesn't need or want to hear, such as the blood trail and gutting the deer— but soon enough they reach the kill site.

The little buck lies brown on the snow. Sarah squints and tries not to look at the caved-in belly, at the blood on the white hair and the spots of red on the snow.

"I saw your dog over there," Miles says, and points deeper into the woods. "He's probably still lurking around."

At the site, Miles kicks at some chunks of fat covered in a thin layer of snow. The white vein-covered gut bag looks like a giant, deflated mushroom.

Still holding her gun, she hunches her shoulders. "Ick."

"It wasn't that bad," Miles says. "I thought for a second I might puke, but I didn't."

"Great," Sarah mutters.

"And it was amazing—the crows were here within minutes!" Miles says.

Brush's tracks are all around the remains; there's a

bare spot where he lay down to eat. She kneels. Puts her palms on the leaves; they are soft but cold. As Miles rattles on about the deer, she looks over her shoulder. One brown ear pokes out from behind a tree. "There he is!" she says.

"Where?" Miles says quickly.

"Promise you won't shoot him?" Sarah says.

Miles pauses. "I won't shoot him."

"Over there, to the right, behind those trees."

Miles swivels around, but Brush's brown head disappears.

"He's afraid of you," Sarah says. She keeps her voice low, her movements slow. "Let me see if I can get closer to him."

"Don't!"

"Why not?" Sarah says. "He used to belong to somebody."

Miles lets out an exasperated breath. "Maybe. But he's surviving on his own. He knows how to find food. If he didn't, he'd be dead by now."

"But he's always out in the cold. Poor Brush."

"Brush?"

"That's my name for him."

Miles shakes his head sideways. "This is stupid. I have to drag the deer home."

"Do you need some help?"

"No. It's not that big, and it slides on the snow. Just be careful around that dog."

"Don't worry—he's not going to bite me."

When Miles is out of sight behind some trees, she kicks loose a chunk of meat. Or fat. Something yucky. Holding it away from her body, she walks to the side, keeping her posture low and nonthreatening. She sits down in the snow where Brush can see her, whispers to him but keeps her eyes downward.

Brush sits up from his crouch and watches. He cocks his square head.

"That's a good dog. Good Brush. Come on, you can do it. Good dog . . ."

His stubby tail wags once—as if it has a brain of its own—then stiffens again. It's as if his friendly tail is not connected to his wary brain. Gradually he eases closer, as slowly as the minute hand on a clock. She keeps murmuring her nonsense conversation; if she looks directly at him, he will stop.

After ten minutes he is almost within arm's length,

but flattened to the ground, ready to bolt. He knows the distance, the length of a human arm with a stick or whip. She sings a song, a baby song she hasn't thought of in years: "Did you ever see a lassie, a lassie, a lassie? Did you ever see a lassie go this way and that?"

For a long second Brush's eyelids droop and his shoulders relax. Continuing to sing, very softly, she eases forward the piece of deer fat. Holds it out to him. Brush's nose quivers, and his eyes cross as the fat comes nearer and nearer to his snout. With a lunge, he darts forward and snaps it from her hand. Sarah falls over backward—if Brush were a rattlesnake, she'd be dead.

The following night for dinner they eat venison. Miles has hung the deer in the sawmill shack, pulled off the skin to cool the carcass, and then cut off some meat. He now stands at the woodstove tending the frying pan. Small, round loin chops, cooking in a mix of butter and wild rice. The skillet throws off a sweet, hot, earthy smell—like the odor of a strange new restaurant.

"Most people cook wild game so they can't taste the wild part," Miles says. "They cover up the taste with bacon, with sauces—anything to disguise the flavor."

It's as if he's hosting a cooking show.

"Where'd you learn how to cook venison?" Nat asks Miles as she sets the table.

"Actually, I read about it at the library," Miles says with a shrug as he tends the skillet.

Sarah swallows, and then again, because the cabin smells so good. And soon they're ready to eat.

"A salute to Miles," Artie says, hoisting an imaginary glass.

"To Miles," Sarah and Nat say, though not as enthusiastically.

As the platter comes around, Nat says, with an apologetic tone, "Mainly wild rice for me, thanks."

"At least try one bite," Artie says.

"I knew someone would say that," she mutters. Carefully she cuts off a small piece of the venison, seared brown on the outside, pale pink on the inside.

They all watch as the fork goes into her mouth.

"Do we have to make such a big deal about this?" Nat asks. She tries to swallow quickly, but her jaw stops. She looks at all of them, then chews. Slowly.

"Well?" Miles asks.

She takes her time, then swallows. Her eyes go to

the platter. "I think I need another piece—just to make sure."

Miles pushes the platter of venison her way. "Eat up. There's plenty more where that came from."

They finish the whole platter except for one piece.

"Last bite, anyone?" Miles asks.

"No, no way," they groan in unison.

"I can't either," Miles says, leaning back from the table.

"Let's save it for Brush," Sarah says.

Even Miles the mighty hunter does not object.

While their parents do the dishes, Miles sits by the woodstove with his feet up.

"After all, I brought home the meat," he reminds them.

Sarah steps outside. The stars are rising. The air has a hard bite of coldness. "Here, Brush! Here, Brush!" she calls softly.

There is rustling near the sawmill shack. Like a ghost, Brush comes forward. He is covered with sawdust, as if he has been burrowing in it to stay warm. She makes sure to look off to the side as she holds out her hand and the meat. This time he is not so anxious; he takes it quickly but without lunging away.

"Good, Brush, good dog." Still not looking directly at him, she touches the top of his head. His hair is cold but smooth. His skull is heavy and wide. She pets him twice before he pulls away. He wags his tail.

"You go to sleep now," she murmurs, and points to the sawdust pile by the shed.

He cocks his head, looks at her sadly, then limps away.

Back inside, Miles is first to ask: "Was our watchdog out there?"

"Yes," Sarah says quickly. "And I petted him."

"Be careful," Artie says. "We don't want any accidents."

"He doesn't bite," Sarah says defensively, with a glance to Miles. "He just eats fast."

"Where was he?" Miles asks.

"Over by the shed."

"Figures," Miles answers. "He smells my deer. That's why I hung it up there—so nothing could get it."

"He's guarding it," Sarah says.

"Yeah, right!" Miles says. He leans back and puts his hands behind his head as he watches them clean the cooking area after supper. With his long hair, fuzzy chin whiskers, and tattered plaid shirt, he looks like a character from a Jack London story about Alaska. He's slightly louder tonight, too, as if at last—finally—he's the boss of the family. Her parents don't seem to notice Miles's new attitude. The whole thing is slightly creepy.

CHAPTER EIGHTEEN

MILES

AFTER THE FIRST REAL SNOW—FIVE inches in one night—Miles motors up to Old But Gold on his Kawasaki. Riding in snow is not his favorite thing. The bike has knobbies, and he stays around thirty miles per hour to avoid skidding, but he leaves behind a narrow black trail on the highway. Light snow is still falling; his tracks should be covered within the hour.

At OBG he steps inside the empty front office, which is hot, full of cigarette smoke, and cluttered floor to ceiling with junk—"collectibles," as they are called: old woodworking tools and cabbage cutters for making sauerkraut, canners and jars. Miles would call them "use-ables," and he could make them all work, thanks to Mr. Kurz's stories of how he lived. He'd already learned how to can venison.

"Howdy, Miles," Butch says from behind him.

"Hey," Miles says.

"Special on eight-track players today."

"Just what I need," Miles says. Butch is not that much older than he is.

"What's up?" Butch asks.

"Looking for a snowmobile."

Butch's dad appears from the back room. "Got plenty of those," he says. "What kind of sled did you have in mind?"

Miles shrugs as if he's in no hurry and maybe not all that serious. "Something late model. Maybe a Polaris or a Cat." That would be Arctic Cat; he has done his research, also at the library.

"Got just what you're looking for," Albert says. "Butch, take Miles in back."

Butch jerks his head for Miles to follow.

The garage adjoining the office is jammed with motorcycles, lawn tractors, fishing boats, trailers, and jumbled piles of sports equipment from guns to hockey skates to snowmobiling gear, along with a whole wall stacked with televisions, old computers, and other electronic equipment.

"Wow," Miles says.

"In bad times people's toys are the first things to go," Butch says.

"No kidding," Miles says.

"My old man's either crazy or a genius," Butch says as he threads his way through a section of riding lawn mowers.

"Probably a genius," Miles says.

"Yeah, well, we need to start selling some of this stuff pretty soon," Butch says. "I keep telling him that, and he says, 'Just wait. Things will turn around. I've been through this before.'"

"That's what all the old-timers say," Miles says.

"Let's hope they're right," Butch says as they arrive at a group of dusty but newer snowmobiles.

Miles climbs onto a lime-green F8 LXR Arctic Cat.

"Nice unit," Butch says.

"Crazy color, plus I need more backseat. For my girlfriend," Miles adds.

Butch gets the joke and wheezes out a brief chuckle. He points to a longer, heavier Polaris. "The Trail Touring

550 has more room for a rider. It's a 2005 model. Very few miles."

Miles climbs aboard. It has a sweet jump seat with a backrest—perfect for his mother or, who knows, maybe even an actual girlfriend someday. As the billboards for the state lottery used to read, "It Could Happen." Miles gives the black Polaris a calculatedly casual look, then moves on. A heavy-duty tow sled—black vinyl with pointed snow nose and trailer hitch, the kind of tub made for serious ice fishing—catches his eye. He pretends that nothing really interests him.

"Got some more sleds coming in this week," Butch says. "Maybe."

"That Polaris back there run all right?" Miles asks. He looks over his shoulder.

"Did when it came in," Butch said. He heads over to it and after some choking to get extra gas into the carb, the Polaris engine coughs several times, then catches. Within seconds the sharp smell of exhaust fills the garage.

Miles signals for Butch to kill the engine, then crouches to examine the track—as with tires, wear is easy to see; its hard rubber is scuffed but not worn.

"Like I said," Butch adds.

"What are you asking for this one?" Miles says.

"Have to talk to the old man," Butch says.

After fifteen minutes of haggling, Miles is about to peel off twelve one-hundred-dollar bills, which would be a good deal; however, before handing over the money he pauses. "Is there a title?"

The old man's eyes flicker toward his son.

"Not sure," Butch says evasively. "I'd have to dig around."

Miles pulls back the wad of bills and puts a pained look on his face.

"How about $900 as is?" the old man says.

"If you throw in a couple of suits, helmets, and that black vinyl tow sled," Miles says.

"Jeez, kid, you're killing me," Albert says with his own pained look. "How about $1,000 for the full package?"

"Deal," Miles says. If he was dishonest, he could tell his folks the higher number and pocket the rest—something he would have seriously considered doing back in the suburbs.

With his motorbike resting in the bottom of the tow sled, and wearing his newish insulated zip-up suit and dark-visored helmet, Miles pulls away from OBG. He cranks the Polaris fast down the empty, snowy highway toward home.

"Yahoo!" he calls. Within seconds he's going seventy miles per hour. At almost 500 cc, the engine has plenty of horsepower. The tow sled starts to whip side to side, and he quickly backs off the throttle; overall it's a sweet ride.

Within ten minutes he's home, where he burns a doughnut in the yard. His parents and Sarah rush out of the cabin.

"Anybody want a ride?" he calls. He unhooks the sled and pushes it to the side.

Sarah and his parents all look at one another. None of them say anything.

"Okay, I'll go first," his mother says. She suits up and puts on the second helmet, and shrieks as they take off.

"It's like the Kawasaki—only faster!" Miles calls back over his shoulder.

Sarah goes last. "Do I have to? It's loud and stinky!" she says. Reluctantly she sits behind Miles and wraps her arms around him.

"Loud and stinky, true, but this winter it's going to save our lives," Miles answers.

She, too, shrieks briefly as he accelerates.

"Hang on!" he calls.

When they return after a short ride, Sarah jumps off. "It's kind of fun, actually. You should learn how to drive it," she says to Nat.

"Me?" Natalie says from the porch. She has been waiting for their safe return.

"Yeah, you. Why not?" Miles asks.

"In case of, I don't know, an emergency," Sarah says, dusting snow from her legs.

"I'm not driving that thing."

Artie comes onto the porch. "Let me drive it," he says.

They all turn to him; it's another one of those meet-the-new-father moments.

"Well, gather 'round," Miles says. "Snowmobile school's in session." He shows them the basics: how to start it, where the brakes are, how to accelerate.

"Can I drive now?" Sarah asks.

Miles gestures toward the front position. Sitting behind, he guides her in a slow loop around the yard and back to the front porch, where she gets off.

"What's the sled for?" Sarah asks, nodding to the side.

"Whatever," Miles answers, scooting forward to the handlebars. "Firewood. Dead animals. Us."

"Us?" his mother asks.

"I mean, if we have to take a family trip to town," Miles says. "Two of us can ride on the machine and two in the sled."

"You're kidding, right?" his mother asks.

"Think of it as a hayride—without the hay," he calls back, then laughs and guns the engine.

"The way you drive that thing, you'd kill us all," Sarah says, backing away.

"Sarah's right—be careful!" Natalie shouts to Miles.

He waves and zooms off, cresting the bank. At the top of his arc, he slips the Polaris sideways like a skateboarder, pivots the rear end, and zips back down the hill. He turns and does it again. His mother disappears into the house, and after his third run, Sarah comes forward and waves her arms.

He skids to a stop. "What?!" he calls.

"You're frightening Emily! And Brush, too. I saw him go running—he'll never come back if you keep roaring around," she shouts.

"Good!" Miles says, and powers up for another run.

His mother comes back onto the porch of the cabin.

"Go do that somewhere else!" she calls. "I can't tell you how annoying it is."

"Fine," Miles says. "See you later." He revs the motor and heads into the woods and down the snowy trails for one last dash through the woods before supper.

CHAPTER NINETEEN

SARAH

AFTER MILES HAS GONE, SARAH looks for Brush, who is nowhere to be seen. She checks the usual spots: the sawdust pile near the sawmill shack, the edge of the brush near Emily's pen, the hill overlooking the cabin. No dog. She shivers. The air is damp and cold in the late afternoon. Snow is falling again. She feeds Emily and, after a last look around the silent yard, heads into the cabin.

"Miles back yet?" her father asks, coming in with another armful of firewood.

"Not yet."

He glances through the window, then kneels by

the stove and tends the fire. Her mother tends to the woodstove—she's making corn bread for dinner. Sarah herself curls up close to the woodstove with a book, one of her old favorite fantasy novels; but she can't concentrate.

She steps into the kitchen area, which is warm and smells good. "Need any help?" she asks her mom.

"Not really, dear," Nat says cheerfully.

Sarah goes to the small window and looks out. The light is grayer still, and the yard is silent and ever smaller because of the thickening snow. No Brush. And no Miles.

She goes back by her mom and perches on a stool. "How did you meet Dad?"

Her mother pauses. She turns to Sarah with a smile—and a glance at Artie, who is lost in his music. "At the university in Minneapolis—I thought you knew that."

"Yeah, yeah," Sarah says impatiently. "But how did it happen?"

"I stalked him," her mother says, stirring the yellow batter with a wooden spoon.

"What?!"

Her mother laughs. "He was in this intro to music class I had to take—what do I know about music?—

and I thought he was cute. Brown, curly hair. Totally absorbed in the lessons. It was like there was no one else in the room except him and the professor. And your dad knew his stuff. He asked questions that no one else had even thought of—including the professor."

"And?"

"And there's nothing like being ignored that makes a woman competitive," her mother says.

"So you made the first move?" Sarah presses.

"You could say that, yes," her mother answers. There is color in her face now; maybe it's the warmth of the kitchen or maybe it's the memory. "The semester was almost over before I mustered up courage. I managed to walk out of class next to him, pretending to be totally confused about that day's lesson."

"You played dumb! No way!" Sarah exclaims.

Her mother picks up on the teasing. "I guess I did, yes. Hey, sometimes we girls gotta do what we gotta do."

"What happened next?"

"That particular day?"

Sarah nods.

"We went to the student union, had coffee, and went over the lesson—it was musical notation, I remember— and he showed me how to tap it out with my fingers."

"That's sort of romantic," Sarah says. She glances at her father.

"I thought so," her mother says. "Especially when he got impatient and said, 'You're not quite getting it. Here, give me your hand.'"

"Whoa," Sarah says.

"Exactly," her mother answers with a sideways glance at her husband. "So he took my hand in his, turned mine palm up, and did this slow, drumming thing on it with his fingers while I read the chart."

"How come you never told me this?" Sarah asks.

Her mother shrugged. "I don't know," she says with a serious look on her face. "I should have. Long ago. Back at home, there was never time."

They are both silent for long moments.

"Anyway," her mother says, "gradually he stopped drumming on my palm, and I stopped looking at the chart. We just looked into each other's eyes."

"And you were still holding hands!" Sarah adds.

"Very good!" her mother says, and laughs.

Sarah looks across the kitchen to her father, then out the little window, to the gray-blue sky. "That kind of thing will never happen to me," she says, and sticks out her lower lip.

"Why of course it will!" her mother says; she drops her spoon into the bowl with a clatter and comes over to wrap Sarah in a big hug.

Sarah begins to sniffle and lets her mother continue to squeeze her. The moment might go on forever but for an odd thudding on the porch, then a scratching on the door.

She and her mother look quizzically at each other.

"Brush?" Sarah asks, and hurries to the door.

But it is Miles. Miles lying there, covered in dirt and snow, with his left foot turned the wrong way.

"Accident." He groans, and slumps in the doorway.

CHAPTER TWENTY

MILES

THE CRASH IS NOT THAT wild. No soaring hang time. No big air over an invisible hump in the trail. No tumbling rollover down the riverbank. Just a low-hanging oak branch covered with snow that he didn't see—then a camera flash inside the bowl of his helmet. *Boom*, like a gunshot, and a rushing sound all in the same instant. Like a roadside bomb that starts with light and sound, then blows him backward on the Polaris seat.

He hits the edge of the jump seat, which flips him up in the air. His left ankle slams another branch, or maybe the ground when he lands—something hard. He has a flash of an icicle falling, breaking—but then it's a tunnel of light closing, a ring of brightness shrinking smaller and smaller to a single black-and-red spot. Then lights-out.

He comes to. Sort of. He's lying on the trail a few yards behind the Polaris, which sits there, idling. He can't move. His eyelids flutter closed, then open again; but the rest of him doesn't want any part of moving.

The snow is soft. That's a good thing. He is lying on his back inside a little snow globe, the shake-up kind; the only thing moving is the slanting, drifting snow above and all around him. A snow kaleidoscope turning and churning up a sick-to-his-stomach swirl of the falling snow. His left leg hurts.

Not badly.

Hurts at a great distance.

Soldiers with missing legs and arms still have pain in the amputated limbs—"ghost pain," it's called—which doesn't seem fair. He has a far-off, separated, distant kind of pain that's already crawling closer. His leg hurts in pricks and pokes—a hurt that streams a tiny message: "I'm comin', and I'm gonna hurt REALLY bad." He concentrates on holding back the big pain as long as possible.

Keeping the big hurt far away.

He vaguely remembers tumbling backward—being swept off the snowmobile as if by a giant broom. He moves his arms, his leg (his good leg); he can feel his spine, his neck; his hands clench and unclench—all of which is a good thing. Everything works except his left leg way below the knee. Best not to move any of that. Best to keep it far away. In another time. Another life.

Then the dam breaks and the pain comes: a surge of cold water filled with razor blades of ice or fire, a spear heated to white-hot iron, then driven into his ankle. A wolf howls nearby, but it's his own animal voice rising to a scream. He has never heard that sound come from his throat, that wail from his body. He flails his head from side to side, reaching up to tear off his helmet, which is cracked across the top like a dropped hard-boiled egg. Not that removing the loser helmet helps lessen the pain. The wolf howls again—which can't be him, because his mouth is full of snow—and then he sees it, to the side, a few yards away: an actual wolf. He blinks. It's not a real wolf; it's the wild dog. Brush. He lowers his muzzle as he ends a short howl.

"You," he whispers to the dog.

Brush watches without expression.

"What do you want with me, you bastard!" He groans. Brush tilts his head slightly as if trying to read his lips.

"You think you've got me now? Well, you don't," Miles adds. He touches his pocket, feels around, and finds his trusty hunting knife. He yanks it free and holds it in the air. "Cut your throat."

Brush has no reaction, and Miles drifts back inside the snow globe, where the world is silent and soft. When he looks again, Brush has shape-shifted; now he sits almost within arm's reach.

Miles jerks up the knife. "Some of this? Come get it," he mumbles. Brush only sits there, staring, without expression. Miles turns his face sideways into the snow— which burns on the surface of his cheek and helps keep him awake. He struggles to one elbow, then two. Sits up. The woods around tilt sideways—someone tipped the snow globe—and Miles closes his eyes to make the trees stop moving. Either the woods are tipped or something inside his head is at the wrong angle. Keeping his eyes shut will not get him back onto the snowmobile.

Get home.

He opens one eye this time. Back in the suburbs, when he was in seventh grade, he and some friends each stole some booze from their parents, mixed it with Mountain Dew, and got drunk. Throwing up, dizzy, never-drink-again drunk. As then, using one eye is best; trying to see with both eyes gives him double vision. Two of everything: two trees, two Polaris snowmobiles waiting to take him home. One eye will get him home—if he can crawl aboard.

He takes a breath. Concentrates. Separates his ankle pain from the rest of his body. Begins to drag himself toward the mumbling Polaris. He's a snow angel fanning slowly backward.

His progress is inches at a time. The broken bone near his ankle follows like an animal caught in a leghold trap; it howls on the inside as it keeps dragging itself forward. He pauses for a short nap but jerks awake and flails outward with the knife, just in case. The dog stays just out of arm's reach.

Miles flashes on the cheesy old black-and-white television series *Lassie*. Lassie the Wonder Dog, who would always save the day. Lassie, who would run back to the cabin, barking wildly, to sound the alarm and bring help to save little Timmy, who is trapped by a rattlesnake in the dry streambed with a rumbling flash flood approaching. If Lassie was here, she would lick Miles's face when he passes out and keep him awake. If Miles was Timmy, he would somehow have a paper and pencil (perhaps he took the long way from school) so he could write a note, tuck it under Lassie's collar, then send her racing home for help.

Brush only watches. His eyes are as blank as gray sky, his mangy brown body as unmoving as a tree stump. With a surge of adrenaline, Miles back-scrabbles close enough to grab the side of the snowmobile. After a deep breath he heaves himself aboard—one lurching motion to compress the pain in the shortest time span possible. . . .

It isn't until he comes to that he realizes he passed out again; and he finds himself sitting upright on the seat, slumped over the dashboard. Below, one foot is pointed forward, the other foot is turned outward. He cracks the throttle partway open and heads down the trail.

Toward home.

He makes it to the yard, parks as close as he can

to the cabin, then considers what to do. He rules out screaming—he doesn't want to scare his family—so he does what any normal person would: crawls off and drags himself up the steps, then raps weakly on the cabin door.

CHAPTER TWENTY-ONE

SARAH

AS THEY ARRIVE AT THE hospital emergency entrance, they look like survivors from the Donner Party. Her father and mother rode with Miles in the tow sled, keeping him propped up and alert, and his leg elevated. The three of them sit immobile, covered with snow spun up by the snowmobile. When Sarah kills the engine, her parents stir like bears emerging from a winter den.

Miles groans—which is a good thing—and Sarah leaps off the machine and hurries inside to get help.

"We've had a snowmobile accident!" Sarah calls. The attendant rings a buzzer, and two people in white hurry out through the swinging doors. "Wheelchair or gurney?" the first one calls.

"Ah, wheelchair probably," Sarah says. "Or maybe not. I don't know!" Her voice breaks; it's as if she has been holding her breath the whole trip.

"Gurney," the other nurse calls, and they hustle toward the entrance.

Outside, her parents are crouched beside the sled holding Miles's hands. "We'll take it from here," the nurses say to Sarah. Within a short minute they slide Miles onto the flat stretcher, then scissor it upright onto its wheels, where it locks with a sharp *clack*.

"Good driving, Goat Girl," Miles mutters as he rolls past.

"Piece of cake," Sarah says.

Sarah's hands are shaking, vibrating; maybe it's from the cold, maybe it's from clenching the snowmobile grips for twenty minutes. Then her whole body starts to shiver.

"Come," her mother says, leading her into the waiting room. Sarah plops down into a soft chair and lets out a long breath. Her dad sits with her, one arm tightly around her, while her mother goes to an office behind them to fill out paperwork.

"What about the Travelers thing?" Sarah whispers suddenly.

"Don't worry, your mother will take care of it. She's good at that kind of stuff," her father says.

After several minutes a doctor comes out. "Miles Newell family?"

They all hurry over.

"He's going to be fine," the doctor says. "But he has a broken ankle and probably a mild concussion. I'm waiting on the X-rays, but it's pretty clear that we'll need to operate on that ankle and put in a pin or two."

Sarah and her parents all look at one another.

"You said a concussion?" Nat asks.

"Maybe. We want to be on guard for a closed-head injury. They're subtle and tricky, so we want to watch him closely for a couple of days."

Sarah and her parents look at one another again.

"Any questions?" the doctor says.

"When will you operate on the ankle?" Art asks.

The doctor glances at his watch. "It'll have to be tomorrow morning. Right now we'll reposition the bones and get his pain under control. He'll be first up for the orthopod in the morning."

"Thanks," Nat says, but the doctor has already turned away.

They look around the waiting room.

"So what do we do now?" Sarah asks.

Artie's cheeks are red from the cold. "One of us should stay with Miles," he says.

"We all should stay—tonight, I mean," Sarah says. "We can camp out here in the waiting room, then in the morning after surgery decide what to do."

"What about Emily? And Brush?" Nat asks. Her mother has taken a liking to the old dog and has been feeding him on the sly.

"They'll be all right for one night alone," Sarah says.

"Okay, we'll stay," her mother says.

They sink onto the couches. Stare at one another. Sarah leans closer to her mother. "Did you have any trouble with"—she lowers her voice—"our 'address' thing?"

"None," her mother says. "I brought it up right away, but they didn't care as long as we had an insurance policy number."

"Do we?" Sarah asks dumbly.

"Yes, dear," her mother says, smoothing Sarah's hair. "That's what parents do."

"I know, I have helmet hair," Sarah says, and leans away from her mother's touch.

"It's not that bad," her mother says.

In the women's room she draws up with a jerk before the mirror. "Helmet hair" is an understatement. Some of her hair is wet and matted; some of it sticks out as if she has a giant tumor. It could use washing, too. With nothing else to do, she decides to take advantage of the hot water, liquid soap, and a hand dryer on the wall. She washes her hair in the sink, scrubs her face, and douses her armpits. When she returns to the lobby, her parents are tipped against each other on a couch and look half asleep. For some reason Sarah is not tired. She settles in with a *Celeb* magazine and catches up on entertainment gossip. Once she glances up at the soft *whirk-whirk-whirk* of a squeaky wheel on a janitor's cart, then returns to the magazine. Her main thought is how insane most women's magazines really are: All they do is make girls and women feel bad about themselves so they'll go out and buy beauty products.

"Sarah?" a boy's voice asks.

She looks up, startled. Pushing a sweeper, which he has paused in midstroke, is a dark-haired kid in white hospital pants and shirt. It's Ray.

MILES

ALL HAIL KING MORPHINE, OR whatever the injection was.
After the doctor pokes the inside of Miles's right arm,
the pain in his ankle recedes. Leg grows longer and
longer—carries his ankle away with it. Ten, twenty, fifty
feet long—one amazing leg that stretches off the bed,
down the hall, and through the door outside, where it
disappears into the falling snow.

He's suddenly warm all over. Warm from the
inside out. Floaty. He hears snatches of songs, trippy
psychedelic bands from the 1960s . . . great time to have
been alive . . . annoyed that he missed it. But he'd be like,

a hundred years old right now. No, not one hundred. More like . . . He can't do the math. Concentrates, but he can't make the numbers stay still. Can't make them stay in columns that he can add and subtract. The numbers float around like lazy black flies—he grabs at them.

"Try to stay still," a woman's voice says; her hands press his arms back down to the blankets.

"Headache," he mumbles.

"I would think," she says. "You cracked your helmet. You need to buy a better one next time."

"Where am I?" Miles asks.

"The hospital. You had a snowmobile crash."

He squints from side to side. Something about the room—maybe it's the smell—reminds him of Mr. Kurz's little room at Buena Vista Convalescent Home. The nurse leans over him and shines a penlight in his eyes. "Can you follow the little light for me one more time?"

"Sure," Miles says, as if it's no big deal; but it takes all his energy to keep up with the slowly moving light. So easy to lose interest. Think of other things. He tries to focus and jerks his eyeballs back to the light.

"Concussed for sure," the nurse murmurs to someone else.

"Let's get some more X-rays," a man's voice says.

Miles can't see much of anything after the light beam clicks off; he closes his eyes. Floats in the warm bath of the painkiller. He can smell himself—he's overheated and suddenly wringing wet under the blanket. The same odor as Mr. Kurz's overly warm room at Buena Vista: old wool, sweat, woodsmoke.

"Hi again," a cheerful voice says above Miles, and the spotlight shines in his eyes. "Could you tell me your name and date of birth?"

He shakes his head to clear it, but the fog doesn't go away. He works his lips to bring up the right words. "Name and birthday?"

"Yes."

"Miles Kurz. February 29, 1920."

CHAPTER TWENTY-THREE

SARAH

"SARAH! WHAT ARE YOU DOING here?" Ray asks.

"My brother!" she says. A sob rises halfway in her throat.

Ray is silent. It's as if he knows better than to ask certain questions in a hospital emergency room.

"Snowmobile accident. He has a broken ankle. Concussion maybe—but he's going to be all right," she says quickly.

"That's great," Ray answers just as quickly, with a glance around the emergency room lobby. "I mean, not great that it happened."

Sarah nods and manages a small smile.

"But great that he's going to be okay. And great to see you! Jeez—," he begins with a pained looked on his face.

Sarah glances over to her parents, both of whom are watching. "This is Ray. From school."

They wave wearily.

Ray quickly steps over and shakes hands with them. "Ray O'Keefe. Sorry about the accident, but the doctors here are really good."

"Thanks," Nat and Artie say.

Ray returns and doesn't make a big deal about meeting her parents, which reminds Sarah of why she likes him: He doesn't think twice (or ten times) about things. He is not, like most eighth graders, terminally self-conscious.

"How long have you been here?" he asks.

"A couple of hours."

He glances to the far side, then tilts his head that way; Sarah follows his squeaky sweeper. There's a corner where they're sort of alone—at least out of sight of her parents.

"So," he begins with his killer smile.

Sarah can only smile back. He always makes her warm all over; her skin glows as if she's in the sauna. "So why'd

I disappear from school?" she asks.

"Mackenzie said you were a Traveler," Ray says. "She blabbed it all over school."

"Great," Sarah mutters.

Ray waits. "Well, are you?" he asks. "I mean, not that I care."

Sarah hesitates—and then in a rush she tells him everything. Well, not everything, but the big things: about being from Minneapolis, about living in a cabin outside of town.

"I knew there was something interesting—something different about you." Ray says.

"I'm going to finish eighth grade through the Alternative Education Center. I pick up my packets once a week, take them home, turn them in the next week. It's pretty boring, but at least I don't have to put up with Mackenzie and her friends."

"I knew that, too," Ray says.

"Knew what?"

"That she and her gang were not your crowd."

"Yeah, well, now I don't have any crowd," Sarah replies.

"Except me," Ray says. He leans closer and touches her clean hair; he lifts it as if to feel its weight.

She swallows; her throat starts to close up.

"So Miles is going to be here a few days?" Ray asks.

"Looks that way."

"How are you and your family going to do this? I mean, will you commute to your cabin? Stay in town?"

"I don't know," she answers.

"How about tonight? Are you hanging here?"

"Yes."

"Good," Rays says. "I get off at ten."

"So?" Sarah says. She regains her wits now that Ray has stopped playing with her hair.

"So, I don't know," Rays says. "Maybe we could hang out."

"Here?" Sarah says.

"No," Rays answers quickly. "There are places. Like Dave's Pizza. It's not that far away. You're probably hungry; we could bring some pizza back to your parents."

"Do you always pick up hungry, vulnerable girls in the emergency room lobby?"

"It's my speciality," Rays says.

"Okay. I'll talk to my parents," she says.

"But I need to keep working right now," Ray adds. "I'll see you back here in a couple of hours?"

She returns to her parents, says nothing for a while,

and pretends to read a magazine while Ray sweeps the floor. When no adults are looking, he plants the sweeper with one hand, then pirouettes around it as if it's a prop in a cheesy dance musical. Sarah giggles.

Her mother blinks. "What?"

"Nothing," Sarah answers. Across the lobby, Ray now works the sweeper in routine strokes, though with a glance toward Sarah.

"Tell me about this Ray," Nat says.

Sarah colors slightly; her mother has great radar. Sarah gives her the full story—about school, how they met on her first day. "And he wants to get a pizza with me when he gets off work," she finishes in a blurt. "We'd bring some back to you. . . ."

"Pizza sounds great," her dad says; she didn't think he was awake.

The two hours until ten P.M. are longer than any day at the cabin. She goes into the bathroom twice to check her hair, and when she comes out the second time, Ray has appeared—with his father, and the two of them are talking to her parents.

"Oh God," Sarah murmurs.

Ray's dad is a normal-looking guy—tall and brown eyed like Ray—and wears the standard nurse's outfit:

loose blue pants and top, a stethoscope draped around his neck, a pager clipped to his waistband. "And this must be the mystery girl!" he says as she arrives. HERB O'KEEFE, his name tag reads.

"Mystery girl?" Sarah asks. Ray rolls his eyes in embarrassment.

"Well, Ray told me about this new girl in school—how she was there and made this, how shall I say, big impression on Ray, and then disappeared."

"Big impression?" Sarah asks Ray.

"I have no idea what my dad's talking about," Ray says, which gets a smile from the adults.

"Anyway," Herb says to them all, "if you need anything, have me paged; you've got a friend here at the hospital."

"Actually, Sarah and I are going to go pick up a pizza for the Newells," Ray says with perfect timing.

"Good idea," Herb says. He shakes hands once more all the way around. "I work until midnight, so I'll stop back and see you folks then."

There's a long moment of dead air.

"Well, I guess we'll go, then," Ray says.

Outside, the snow is falling heavier now.

"How far is it?" Sarah asks, her breath fogging in the chilly air.

"A few blocks," Ray says.

"So let's drive," Sarah says.

"Drive?" Ray asks.

Sarah points to the snowmobile and hands Ray the cracked helmet. "It's the only extra we've got," she says. Ray puts on the helmet and climbs behind Sarah. His long legs clamp alongside her hips and keep her warm. His arms loop around her waist. Actually, higher—just under her breasts; even with her winter jacket on, she can feel them resting on his arms, and she knows he can feel them, too.

"You told me you were a city girl," he says in her ear. "Where'd you learn how to drive a snowmobile?"

"I'm a natural," she says.

"I agree," he says, and holds her tighter.

Dave's Pizza is warm, cheesy smelling, a bit dim, and totally 1970s with its booths and black-velvet wall art. She follows Ray to a corner booth; they sit across from each other, knees touching.

"Sorry again about Miles," Ray begins.

Sarah winces. "We told him to be careful. It was his first day with the snowmobile."

"I've never driven one," Ray says. "We're kind of a limited-spark-plugs family. My dad says that life is better the fewer the spark plugs you're responsible for. We don't even mow our lawn, which really annoys our neighbors."

A waitress comes and takes their order. "There's no pepperoni today," she says before either Ray or Sarah can speak.

"But lots of cheese, right?" Ray asks.

The waitress stares.

Sarah giggles.

"How about sausage?" Ray asks the waitress.

"Yes. But you get it only on small- or medium-sized pies."

"Okay, we'll have two mediums with extra sausage," Ray says.

"We don't do extra sausage."

Sarah holds back another giggle.

"Okay," Ray says. "Then we'll have three small pizzas."

"With sausage," the waitress says; she's totally annoyed with them.

"Yes—if that's okay with you," he says quickly to Sarah.

"Sure," Sarah says. "We're all carnivores now."

The waitress stalks off. And the pizza takes a long time to arrive, which is fine by Sarah. What else does she have to do? They talk about everything. She doesn't know quite when it happened, but they are holding hands across the tabletop. When the pizzas finally come, they're in three boxes—as if the waitress wants them gone.

"Let's eat ours here!" Sarah says, squeezing Ray's hands before she lets go.

"You sure?" Ray says. "You parents might be hungry."

"Another half hour won't kill them," she says.

"Well, you're the driver," Ray answers.

"Yes, I am," Sarah says, and leans forward to give him a quick kiss.

"Whoa!" Ray says.

It's the best pizza date she has ever had, mainly because it's her first one.

Ray eats quickly, as if he's really hungry—especially for pieces of sausage. "Sorry," he says, realizing that she's watching. "We don't get much meat, so I kinda pig out when I get a chance."

"Your parents are vegetarians?" she asks.

"Sort of but not really. They'll eat meat, but they have to know where it comes from. They won't buy any meat that comes from a factory farm—which rules out meat from the supermarkets. We used to have a local farm connection, but that's all screwed up now."

"Do you eat venison?"

"For sure. A friend of ours was driving, and he saw a car hit and kill this deer. Another car stopped, and the two guys almost had a fight over the dead deer. But my friend got it, threw it in his trunk, took it home, butchered it, and then gave us some. I know roadkill sounds gross, but it was really tasty."

"If you want more venison, I'll get some for you," Sarah says. Where that came from she doesn't know; the words just fell from her mouth.

"Do you hunt?" Ray asks with surprise.

"Sure. It's no big deal," she says with a shrug.

"Sweet," Ray replies. "You, I mean."

She blushes, and they hang at Dave's another half hour until Ray says, "We really really should get back to the hospital. My dad will be getting off soon, and your parents will be starving."

"So you need a ride?" Sarah teases.

"Ah, yes. Please?"

"You have to hold the pizza box."

"Which means I can't hold on to you?"

"Sorry," she says.

But Ray figures out how to do both. He wraps his

arms around her and holds the pizza on her lap; she wishes his arms were free, like before.

At the emergency room entrance they hurry in with pizza—and her mother jumps up in relief.

"Sorry, it was really busy," Sarah say.

"Right," Nat says with a glance at Ray.

"If the pizza is cold, there's a microwave in the little kitchen over there," Ray says helpfully.

"Any news on Miles?" Sarah asks.

"He does have a concussion, the doctor said."

Sarah sucks in a breath. "What does that mean?"

"We don't know yet. He can come home, but for sure he's going to have to take it easy—not do anything for a while," her mother says. Her eyes are serious and slightly scared.

"Don't worry, we can manage," Sarah says quickly— with a glance toward Ray.

CHAPTER
TWENTY-FOUR

MILES

NAPS.

Lots of naps, between which he reads old Garfield comics. They're the only reading material he brought from home, and they're just right again. Not too many words.

His naps stretch over many days. Naps like bear dens or little caves that he crawls inside. Sometimes he wakes to find Herb O'Keefe, the nurse, talking to him. Examining his ankle.

"How are you doing today, Miles?" O'Keefe asks.

"Great," Miles answers. Today the annoying Ray

O' Keefe is standing behind his father.

"Hey," Ray says cheerfully.

Miles ignores him. Nat hovers in the background; his father is outside. The main part of the cabin is not big enough for everybody.

"Your dad's out chopping firewood," Nat says. "Either that or throwing his axe."

"Cool," Miles says. He sometimes hears his father's axe: *thoop!* and then *thoop!* again, in a steady rhythm. Once he awoke and mistook the sound for his own heartbeat thudding in the pillow at only a few beats per minute, as if he really was a hibernating bear.

"Miles?" Herb asks.

"Hey," he says, and refocuses. Best to be as normal and as cheerful as he can around Herb. When he's honest about the headaches and the brain fog, the guy hangs around longer. Asks more questions. Miles is still wearing an ankle cast, though the soft kind with hook-and-pile straps to keep it tight. Using a cane, he has been able to move about the cabin and onto the front porch. He can't ride the snowmobile, chop wood, or hunt—any sudden movements and his headache comes back like a needle poking deep inside his brain. His family has to do all the work now. The guarding, too.

"Christmas was good?" Herb asks, carefully opening the ankle brace.

"I don't remember," Miles says.

Herb glances sideways to Miles's mother.

"Joke!" Miles says to them.

"Yeah, well . . . ," his mother says, and trails off. She suddenly looks older—there are gray threads in her hair—and her face is thinner, too.

Herb hasn't laughed either. "So what'd you get?"

"Mean for Christmas?"

Herb nods as he carefully massages Miles's ankle.

"New snowmobile helmet," he answers. "Sarah's wearing it until I'm back in the saddle."

"That's the spirit," Herb says.

Ray clears his throat, then speaks up. "Ah, is Sarah around, by the way?"

"She's outside," Nat says.

"Fishing. Should be," Miles says. "Probably in the spear house. Upriver."

"Don't worry, son, we've got plenty of food," Nat says.

"I'm here, too, as a backup—I deliver groceries," Herb says.

"The idea was . . . we do it ourselves," Miles says,

turning to his mother.

"But you have friends now," Herb explains. "Our family is happy to help yours."

"Don't need help!" Miles exclaims, then squints from a sudden arrow of pain inside his head.

"Please—come lie down, Miles," his mother calls; he lets her help him into the kids' bedroom. There, in the cool semidarkness, he pulls a blanket over himself and concentrates on thinking nothing at all. Beyond the thin, wooden wall his mother and Herb murmur.

"—should see a neuropsychologist," Herb says. "There's a good one I know who rotates through our hospital."

His mother says something Miles can't make out.

"Some tests would probably give us a better idea of what he needs," Herb says.

"—needs more rehab than staying quiet in a dark room," she says.

"I agree. I'm not a doctor," Herb says, "but Miles has symptoms in common with people who have migraines. Bright lights, sudden movement, major changes in temperature—all those things can trigger the headache."

"But what if it's more than just a headache?" His

mother's voice falters at the end.

"Well, that's what we need to find out," Herb says.

There's a long pause. "Can I make you a cup of coffee?" Nat says. "That, at least, I know how to do."

There's a pause. "Sure," Herb says. "Ray and Sarah probably won't mind."

"Yes, those two," Nat answers in a what-can-I-say voice.

There's silence, during which Miles drifts off. He blinks awake only seconds later—at least he believes it to be seconds.

"—chopping and splitting wood with his axe. He's gotten quite good at it," Nat says. Her voice has changed; it's like some time has passed. "For Artie, it's something concrete."

"Caregiving is concrete," Herb says. "You just can't see the results like you can with a stack of firewood."

"Could you drive Miles to town?" his mother says. "I mean, when we get an appointment?"

"Sure. I'll check the doctors' schedules tomorrow," Herb says. The conversation continues about the weather, the climate predictions (more sunshine all the time). Yeah, right! Coffee cups clink, and then there are thumping sounds as his father returns with wood. A blast of cold air from outdoors. Clank of the stove door, squeak of the damper inside the stovepipe. Adult talk continues. There is a fine line between brain damage and boredom, so Miles allows himself another little nap.

SARAH

BRUSH, WHO'S IN THE LITTLE spear house with Sarah, lifts his head from the thin floorboards.

"What?" Sarah says.

He growls—a low rumble.

"It's just ice noise," Sarah says. "Don't worry about it." They are upriver from the cabin, in a bay where the ice is thicker and safer. The cramped, dark house is situated at the edge of the wild rice bed, where northern pike cruise, looking for baitfish. She works her red-and-white decoy fish in the water below. The glowing hole is like a television in the floor but with a blank screen.

A luminous, pale square of light. A spear (Mr. Kurz's) leans against her right shoulder, and its retrieve cord is tied to the wall. The skinny iron rod, about four feet long, ends in a wide hand of five sharp tines. She keeps the spear close by the open hole in the ice, which is a smooth, glowing, blue-white slab about a foot deep. She's ready but has seen no fish.

The only entertainment is the talking ice—intermittent groans, ripping and booming noises that used to scare her, but now she understands them. It's not the ice breaking; it's the ice growing. Thickening. Getting stronger. In the last few days, when the temperature has fallen to twenty below zero, she has had to chip away several inches of new ice in order to keep the spear hole open. Fish are skittish during loud ice days; even minnows flinch and dart away when the ice speaks.

Inside the tiny shack it is dark except for a candle for a bit of warmth; Brush is the spear house heater. She couldn't stand the cold in here if not for his big body. He's gotten mostly used to her—though not to anybody else. He'll never be a house pet, but he makes a good spear house dog.

He's restless, however; he cocks his good ear—and

growls again. He sits up, and soon Sarah hears footsteps crunch on snow, growing louder as they approach. Her left hand goes to the shotgun in the corner; her right hand goes to the little sliding peephole board.

The figure approaching is backlit by sun—it's a bright day, maybe another reason that the fish aren't moving—and she squints one eye to see better. Slips a shell into the chamber and gets ready to step outside.

"Ahoy in the spear house!" a voice calls.

"Ray!" she says suddenly.

Brush growls for real this time.

"Stop that," Sarah says.

He quickly lowers his ears, and she opens the door and shoos him outside; then she yanks off her stocking cap and tries to fluff up her hair.

"Are you in there, Sarah?" Ray calls.

"Yes! Come on in," she answers. She swings open the little plywood door, and Ray bends low to step inside. She quickly closes the door behind him.

"Whoa—I'm blind!" he says, and stumbles against her old wooden bench.

"It takes a while for your eyes to adjust," she says with a laugh. "Don't worry, I won't let you fall in the hole."

"Thanks!"

"We have to share my bench, though," she says, scooting over.

He gets situated closer beside her and leans forward to look down. His breath steams above the greenish light from the ice hole. He turns to her, smiles, gives her a quick kiss on the cheek.

"Your dad's doing his thing with Miles?" Sarah asks as she leans against him.

Ray nods.

"How does he seem today?"

Ray shrugs slightly. "Better, I think. Just a couple of slips into Mr. Kurz-world, though you never know when he's kidding."

"Tell me about it," Sarah says.

"And you?" Ray asks. He puts an arm around her and pulls her closer—a friendly, one-armed hug—and anyway, they're both wearing gloves and big parkas.

"The fish must be sleeping today," Sarah says.

"That's not what I meant," Ray says.

"My parents are really worried about Miles," she blurts.

They are silent for a long time. "When this is all over, you could write a book," Ray offers.

"Suburban Chick Turns Woodswoman," Sarah mutters.

"Meets northern boy who doesn't hunt," Ray adds.

She manages a tiny smile.

"Actually, my family could go for some red meat," Ray says.

Sarah glances at him.

"I mean, if you're out hunting someday," he says with a shrug.

"No problem," Sarah says.

And suddenly they're kissing—hard, fumbling kisses in the tight space, with no room to move. They hold each other until her heart slams like a bass drum and she is sweaty all over beneath her winter parka. For some reason she opens one eye to look down at the green square hole in the ice—and quickly pushes Ray away.

"I'm sorry!" he says.

"No—not that. I saw a fish. A northern! A really big one!" She quickly lifts the decoy fish string—makes the little wooden fish dart.

"Oh no, it's my fault!" Ray says.

"Shhhh," Sarah says. "He might come back."

But in the next minute or so he doesn't.

Gradually they relax. "There's always next time," she says. They are silent; it's as if neither knows what to say about the kissing.

"Spearing decoys are cool," Ray says.

"This one's new," she says, hoisting it closer to the surface. "We made it."

"How'd you know how?" Ray asks.

"Miles," she answers."

"Duh," Ray replies.

"It was kind of fun, actually," Sarah says. "Especially the wood carving."

"If the decoys are wooden, what keeps them from floating up to the surface?" Ray asks.

"They're weighted with lead. After you carve them, you drill out a hole in the belly, then pour hot lead inside."

"And the fins?"

"Cut from tin cans, then stuck into the wood with little nails." She lifts the decoy still closer to the surface so Ray can see it better. "You just bend the tail fin a half turn, and that makes the fish turn in a circle." She demonstrates, which is when the big pike, jaws wide and gills flared, lunges back at the decoy.

"Jeez!" Ray shouts, and almost tips over backward on the bench.

"Stay still!" Sarah whispers. "He missed the decoy—

which means he'll circle back."

"It was huge!" Ray breathes. "Looked like an alligator!"

"At least ten pounds," Sarah whispers. "Here—you handle the decoy and I'll get ready with the spear."

"What do I do?"

"Nothing. Let it hang there but be ready to jerk it away if he tries to bite it."

The gray torpedo drifts in from a different direction this time, finning slowly toward the motionless decoy. His beady eyes focus on its colors, and his wide gills fan slowly in and out. Sarah carefully lowers the spearhead and its needle-sharp points, then thrusts it hard—a powerful, jabbing throw. The tines nail the pike just behind his head.

"You got him!" Ray shouts.

"Not yet!" Sarah shouts. She grabs the retrieve cord, which is tied to the end of the spear, and slows down the run of the fish. When the cord grows slack, she pulls it in, hand over hand. The fish is not a fighter or a flopper; the center tine has hit him in the spine, and he comes in quivering and heavy.

"Open the door," Sarah calls to Ray.

He fumbles with the latch, and the sunlight floods in.
"You go out first!" she calls.

Ray vamooses, and, with a grunt, she heaves the dripping, heavy pike from the hole and pitches him onto the snow. Scales as big as quarters glint on the spear tines.

"I can't believe it!" Ray says. "You got him. I could never have done that."

"Sure you could," Sarah says. Even as they look, a film of ice glazes over the shiny green-and-white-spotted sides of the northern pike. Sarah's heart is pounding.

"Now what?" Ray says.

She wants to go back into the spear house with Ray and forget about fishing. But she says, "If we leave the fish outside, Brush will eat it."

Ray shivers. "We'd better head back. The fish will be frozen as hard as a rock within five minutes."

The drag him, tied by a twine looped through his gills and out his mouth, across the snowy edge of the river and onto land. Brush limps along close behind. Sarah has to be on guard that he doesn't bite the fish, but soon they arrive at the cabin.

"Supper is served," Sarah announces as they come inside the cabin; she hoists up the big northern pike.

"My God!" Nat says.

"Wow," Artie says, and Herb O'Keefe begins to clap.

Miles can only smile at the big fish and Sarah. "That's my sister," he says to everyone. It's a cool moment, even though he's looking at her oddly, as if he doesn't quite recognize her. As if he's saying it to convince himself.

CHAPTER TWENTY-SIX

MILES

SARAH DRIVES THE SNOWMOBILE. HE hangs on to her from behind. Riding on the jump seat is totally annoying, but at least he's not stuck in the sled with his mom and dad. It's a bright, cold day in early January; tiny crystals of frost glitter in the air like little pinpricks of light. They are heading into town for his appointment with a visiting neuropsychologist. But first they have to catch their ride.

"Maybe he won't come," Miles says against the side of her helmet.

"Of course he'll come," Sarah calls back.

"Ray, too?" Miles

Sarah turns her face sideways. "Why don't you like Ray?"

"Watch the trail!"

She does.

"Not sure. Never thought you'd have a boyfriend."

"Thanks a lot," Sarah says.

"That came out wrong," Miles says. "Never thought you'd be . . ."

"A big girl?" Sarah finishes.

"Yeah. Big."

"Well, get used to it," Sarah says. She cracks the accelerator just enough to get a shriek from her mother and to make Miles grab on tighter.

"Stop that!" her mother calls from behind.

"Cool," Miles says as she drives on through the snowy woods.

The O'Keefe vehicle is waiting at the highway. An older Dodge minivan with a Blue Star sticker plus hospital parking tags. Windows mostly frosted over except for a thawed oval on the windshield. Black melted spot on the snow beneath the tailpipe.

"See? Told you," Sarah said.

"Yeah, yeah," Miles says crabbily. "Stop here. Park in

the woods, out of sight. We walk down the bank. Be sure to cover your tracks."

They do, then all pile into the O'Keefes' van. Miles sits up front, Nat and Artie in the next seat, and Ray and Sarah in the far back. They cozy up together under a lap blanket. It's sickening.

"Great to see the sun!" Herb says cheerfully as they motor off. "Right, Miles?"

"Not really," Miles says. He's wearing sunglasses against the light. Light kills him—it's like little needles poking into his brain.

"Anyway," Herb says, "you're going to like Dr. Chadron. She's lively, fun, and very sharp."

"Like me," Miles says.

No one says anything.

"Joke," Miles says. His headache is a tiny motor in a far corner of his brain. Idling. Always there. He scrapes frost on his side window so that he can see out. See where they're going. It feels good to be moving. To be on the road again.

At the clinic, which adjoins the hospital, he waits with his family in a small examining room. He has never been claustrophobic until today. He concentrates on reading the wall posters that have generic information about the skull. The brain locked inside it. His mother hums nervously and his father taps.

"Knock-knock!" says a foreign-sounding voice. The doctor is young and pretty in a dark-eyed, silk-scarf-loose-over-her-hair, Muslim kind of way. There's something to be said for women without tattoos or piercings, or a lot of bare skin.

"The Newells?" she says.

Nat nods. "That's us. And this is Miles."

Miles shoots his mother an annoyed look.

"Hello, Miles," the doctor says cheerfully; she has small fingers but a very strong grip. Then she sits and turns sideways in her desk chair as she types something into her computer. Long black skirt, thin and silky. Great ankles. After some chitchat and background about the accident, she opens a notebook. "Okay, Miles, we're going to do a few cognition exercises."

Miles glances at his family. Sarah, mother, father—all stuck in the same room.

The doctor says, "I'm going to read you some things—directions, actually. You try to remember as many as you can. Then repeat them back to me."

Sarah giggles.

"Excuse me?" the doctor says.

"Sorry," Sarah says quickly. "It's sort of an inside joke with our family. Memory Boy, I mean . . ." She trails off.

The doctor pauses a moment, then moves on. "In my field, memory is a key indicator of neuro health," she says, turning to Miles.

"Hit me," Miles says.

"Pardon me?" the doctor says.

"I mean, give them to me. I'm ready."

The doctor glances once more at the family, then begins. "We head north on Elm Street, take a left turn on Second Avenue, and cross the railroad tracks. Then we turn right on Jefferson Street." She pauses to look at him. Walnut-brown eyes, pencil-drawn eyebrows, the silk head scarf. Her slightly weird English. Pink lipstick and great teeth.

"That's it?" Miles asks.

"Yes. Could you repeat them to me?" she asks.

Miles nails it exactly.

"Good. Now another one, longer this time." This route includes two intersections, a bridge, and two stoplights.

He shrugs—nails it again word for word.

"Very good," she says, "though it was a left turn at the last stoplight."

He blinks. "Are you sure?"

"Yes." She leans over to show him the chart. She jots some notes on her pad; Miles frowns and glances at his family.

"Give me the next page," Miles says quickly. "Harder directions."

"All right," she says evenly.

This time Miles closes his eyes and really concentrates.

"Very fine," she says when he recites the route, "though you transposed the bridge and the tunnel."

There is silence in the room. "Are you sure?" Miles asks.

"Yes," she says, a trace of annoyance in her voice. "I use these charts all the time. They're not easy."

"Give me your hardest one!" Miles blurts.

"Excuse me?"

"The toughest one, the most turns—I want to try it."

She pauses, then shrugs. "All right. If you wish. But don't be surprised if you—"

"Go ahead, I'm ready," Miles says, and leans forward on his chair.

She stares at him, then begins. It's a half minute's worth of directions that, like words in a spelling bee, get funkier and more complicated as they go along.

Miles scrunches his forehead, feeling his eyebrows bunch together over his nose, as he listens to the doctor read. He can see the streets, the signs, the turns, the exit numbers; inside his head he strings them together, one by one. The route goes outward, then comes gradually back around, turn by turn, a crazy pattern that gradually reveals its logic: The trip ends where it began.

Keeping his eyes closed, he repeats them in order—until he hits a complicated intersection. He can see it but can't make the correct turn. He tries again, then again, but his tongue can't say the words.

"Damn!" he says, and slumps backward in his chair.

"That's really quite good, Miles!" the doctor says. "You got halfway through level twelve—the most difficult chart."

"No, not good!" Miles says. He looks to his family. Sarah is white-faced and scared, his father grim; his mother tries not to cry.

"I assure you it is," the doctor says. "Most people can't make it through level six—half of what you can remember."

"I don't think you understand," Nat says, then begins to sniffle big-time. "Miles is not 'most people.'"

"Just tell me," Miles says to the doctor. "Do I have all my marbles?"

"Marbles, yes," she says with a trace of a smile. "But concussions are all different. Yours might take some time to heal, but gradually your headaches should go away."

"That's it?" Nat asks.

His family all look at one another.

"Sometimes I wish I was a surgeon," the doctor says to them with an apologetic smile. "You come to me with a broken ankle, I put pins in it, and you're fixed. But head injuries are not like that."

"Is there anything else we can do?" Nat asks.

"As you know, I'm not a regular doctor here. Once a month I visit several hospitals in the area. My home base is in Minneapolis, and it would be really good if Miles were closer to a bigger medical center. I'd like to do more tests."

Miles's parents look at each other.

"But that's up to you," she says. "These are difficult times right now, for all of us."

After the doctor's appointment they borrow the O'Keefe van and head downtown with Ray, who is getting off his shift. The van and its Blue Star sticker make them feel totally local and legal. They have lunch at the World Harvest Café on Beltrami Avenue, which Ray recommends. It's run by young hippies, including a big girl cook who wears a red bandana and a very tight T-shirt with no bra.

"No meat or fresh greens," the counter guy says with a smile. He has an eyebrow stud and a ponytail.

"What's the special?" Art asks.

"Three bean soup. And some great bread," the guy says.

They order, then take their time eating bean soup with a side of cheese and warm wheat bread. As usual, Ray and Sarah are giggling and trying not to paw each other.

Maybe it's the soup, but Miles's headache suddenly lifts. He's not even annoyed by Ray and Sarah, who think he doesn't know that they're holding hands under the table.

After lunch they head over to the library so Nat can do her work thing.

"What about your school packets?" Art asks Miles. "I'll walk over to the AEC with you."

There's a pause.

"Or not," his father says.

Miles swallows. "I can't really . . . read that well right now."

"Brain injury—another lame excuse for not going to school," Sarah says.

Miles manages a half smile.

"Sarah—that's not funny!" Nat says.

"Sorry, bro. I guess it wasn't," Sarah mumbles.

"It was funny," Miles says. "Sort of."

Artie turns to Sarah. "You, on the other hand, have no excuse."

"I know, I know! I'm headed to the AEC right now."

"I'll go with her," Ray says.

"Don't help her with her packets," Miles calls to Ray.

Later, after work, Herb gives them all a ride back to the snowmobile.

"How'd it go with Dr. Chadron?" he asks first thing. There is silence.

"Dr. Chadron is very sweet—," Nat begins.

"She says that Miles needs more tests. Ones that he can't get here," Artie interrupts. There's something in his voice that makes everyone pay attention.

Nobody says anything, and the tone in the van is different after that.

When they arrive at the drop-off point, Herb says,

"I'll wait to make sure your snowmobile starts."

"It'll start," Miles says. He leads the way through the snow.

"Wait, I'll do it," Sarah says, and cranks over the engine. The electric start is sluggish from several hours in the cold, but the motor catches and puffs a cloud of blue smoke.

They say good-bye to Ray and his father.

"Date's over," Miles says to Sarah.

"Shut up," she says as she takes the driver's position; Miles climbs on behind, with Nat and Artie in the sled. They don't seem to mind.

"I'm tired," he says, and leans against her back.

"We're almost home, bro," she says.

Halfway back to the cabin, she sits up straighter on the seat. "Did you feed Brush this morning?" she calls back to her mother.

"No, I thought you did," she answers.

"You should stop feeding him at all," Miles says.

As they arrive at the hilltop above the cabin, Sarah screams; Miles lurches upright behind her to see what's going on.

Below, in the yard, Brush is crouched over Emily. Who is dead. Dead and partially eaten. The dog has broken into Emily's pen, killed her, and dragged her out; and now he is eating her.

Sarah lets out a howl and accelerates down the hill. They scramble off the snowmobile and out of the sled, shouting at the dog, who does not let go of Emily's carcass. They scream and throw sticks, snow—anything—at him; but he growls and drags Emily backward. Toward the woods.

"Get a gun!" Miles calls.

"I will," Sarah answers.

She hurries back from the cabin with her .410, fits a slug into the chamber, and jacks the bolt shut. As she steps forward, the dog growls at her. Keeps tugging at Emily. His yellow eyes are fixed on Sarah, who raises the gun. Nat—but not Artie—turns away.

Toom! Sarah jerks backward from the recoil, and Brush yelps and tumbles in a churning brown heap on the snow. She fits another shell into the chamber and shoots him again in the head—finishes him off. He goes limp. The light goes out of his old yellow eyes. Sarah hands the gun to Miles and disappears into the cabin.

That night the cabin is very warm, and there is supper on the table. Nat goes to the bedroom door and taps lightly. "Dinner?" she calls to Sarah.

Sarah eventually appears, red-eyed and with a blotchy face and bed hair.

It's quiet around the dinner table.

"Hey," Miles says to Sarah.

She only stares at her food.

"Could be the brain damage talking," Miles says, "but you're an amazing sister."

SARAH

IN THE MORNING THEY ARE having breakfast: oatmeal and coffee.

"What did you do with Emily?" Sarah finally says, glancing through the small window toward the yard.

"I put her in the sawmill shack, where nothing would bother her," Miles says.

"I want to bury her," she says.

Miles looks pained. "Ah, the ground is frozen."

Sarah eats another spoonful of oatmeal, then wipes her eyes. "Okay. I'll take her far out into the woods and make a place for her."

Miles glances at the milk jar. There is only a little bit of milk left.

"You can have it," she says.

"No, you should have it," Miles says. He slides the jar her way.

"I can't," she says, and pushes it back.

Outside, with his breath steaming in the sharp, bright air, Miles has loaded Emily into the tow sled. He has turned Emily so that her good side is up. So that the half-eaten side is not visible.

"She's frozen stiff," Miles says.

They look at her. "At least her eyes are closed," Sarah replies.

"You sure you don't want me to come along?" Miles asks.

"No. I'll be fine."

"Take your gun," he says. "You never know."

With the tow sled behind and the .410 alongside Emily, she idles down the trail away from the cabin and through the woods. A funeral procession. There's no hurry. It's a matter of respect.

She drives a half mile deeper into the forest, and where the trail becomes impassable with brush, she stops and kills the engine. Pulling the sled by hand, she goes deeper still into the woods and upward, on a side hill covered with red oak trees. These trees still have their leaves, something she never thought about before; the reddish tan leaves are dead, but they hang on. Each one looks like a little hand with stubby fingers.

She unloads Emily, who is not heavy, and covers her with snow. Then more snow, a tall mound of it. After that she arranges sticks and dead branches like a tepee. More and more sticks until there's a perfect cone with Emily inside. When the snow melts, the branches will slowly come down to cover her.

When Sarah's done making the big pile, she's warm and sweaty. Then, cradling her gun, she sits down, leans back against the mesh of branches, and has a cry. No blubbering, just some silent chest heaving and a few tears. She sits there a long time, thinking about things. If she leaves now, the Emily part of her life is over, so she just sits there and stares across the woods. . . .

A wink of light among the oaks makes her blink. She leans forward and squints. A patch of brown, then another—and a brief pale glint near the ground. Antlers. A huge deer with antlers low to the ground is easing silently among the oaks! He sniffs, paws beneath a tree, then lifts his head suddenly to look and listen behind—

and afterward resumes his slow forward motion.

She tightens her grip on the .410. The snowmobile is behind Emily's funeral mound, and Sarah is hunkered low against the tangled branches. Careful not to make a sound, she shrinks even lower. If he keeps coming, the buck will pass below her on the side hill about the length of a tennis court away. Whatever that is (she should know that distance—so many things back then that she never thought about!).

The buck's body is tan and long, and thickens through the chest and neck. His antlers look fake—too tall and too perfect—like a stick-built headdress. Like a rocking chair screwed atop his head. Her heartbeat begins to slap inside her ears. When the buck dips his head again, she raises her gun and rests it over a knee. Puts her right cheek tight to the cold wooden stock. The buck lifts his shiny, spiky headdress and moves forward. He walks without sound—does not keep his head down for more than a few seconds. He keeps looking behind him.

And then he reaches the open spot below her; she takes a close aim, her right eye as low over the barrel as she can hold it . . . sights on his thick neck . . . and squeezes the trigger.

Nothing!

Squeezes harder—still nothing. She draws a breath, then eases up her thumb to nudge the safety button.

The buck freezes; his white tail goes up and begins to flicker. He looks directly at her.

Boom!

The buck flinches—then bounds away at full speed.

"Oh, my God!" she breathes. It's like a real prayer—or an antiprayer. It's not like she thought she could hit him—or kill him—but at least she tried. It's something to tell Miles, and maybe, someday, her friends, whoever they will be. Not that anyone will believe that she shot at a giant buck.

She stands up in order to take some slow breaths—it's crazy how fast her heart is beating. Below her the hillside is empty but for snow and red oaks. Setting the gun against the funeral mound, she walks down to the deer trail. She just wants to see his tracks. To make sure she didn't dream the big buck.

The leaves are scuffed where he has pawed—and then his tracks disappear as if he has flown away. Which he has, sort of: His next scuff marks in the snow are several yards from the trail—like a world record long jump across the snow—and then again and again, this running track disappearing into the forest. About to turn away, her gaze falls to a red berry in the snow. It's a cranberry, like the ones Miles picked earlier this fall; she looks around, but there are no cranberry bushes, which grow beside water anyway. On the snow are two more specks. Then another. Blood!

"Oh no!" she says.

The little blood spots are like crumbs. Red bread crumbs. She hurries forward to the next, and the next. The trail becomes easier to follow. Dots turn to blotches, then a fine spray every few feet. Head down, she hurries along through the forest, which is now brushier. In places the blood trail is like a spilled cherry snow cone.

She hears a short scream—her own voice—and she jumps backward. The big buck is lying down just ahead in the brush. She crouches low—as if to what? The buck does not move. She watches it for a really long minute, then creeps forward.

The buck lies long and brown on the snow, outstretched, antlers curving up.

Motionless.

She finds a long stick and, holding it with both hands, touches the deer on his leg. Nothing. Holding the stick at the ready, she leans forward to look at the buck's face. Its skyward-looking eye is open and unblinking. She carefully reaches out with a bare hand and touches his heavy antler, which is cold and thick in her hand. Then she sits in the snow beside the big, silent animal and covers her face.

On the snowmobile she heads back to the cabin, at first slowly, then with increasing speed. She flies down the hill like Miles would have—skids to a stop by the porch.

"What's wrong?!" her mother asks with alarm as Sarah bursts into the cabin.

"I got one!"

"Got what?" Artie asks.

"A deer!" she calls.

Miles appears from the bedroom; he looks half asleep. "Say again?"

"Get your coats," she says to her family. "We have a deer to bring home."

"No way!" Miles says groggily. He squints against the light from the doorway.

"It's true," Sarah says. "A buck." She checks her gun to make sure it's unloaded, then leans the .410 in the corner. Its work is done for today.

"Did you dress it out?" Miles asks.

Sarah freezes. "You mean, like, take the guts out?"

Miles nods—then winces and puts both hands to his temples.

"No! I didn't even think about that," she answers.

They are all silent. Miles makes no move to put on his winter coat.

"I'll do it," Art says.

They look at him in surprise.

"No. I can. Just give me a minute," Miles mumbles.

"You stay here," Art says. "That's an order."

Miles blinks in surprise.

"Yes. Listen to your father," Nat adds as she bundles up.

"We can do this," Sarah says; she crosses the wooden floor and gently pushes Miles back toward his sleeping bag. He doesn't resist.

Outside, she fires up the snowmobile. "Hurry—hop on," she calls. Her mother quickly claims the jump seat, while Art takes the sled. "You won't believe how big the deer is! Miles is going to be amazed."

"How do we gut a deer?" her mother asks.

"I kinda know," Sarah says. "Miles told me all about it the first time he did it."

"I'm sure he did," Nat says.

Sarah accelerates forward to make the hill and then

follows her own track deep into the woods toward the dead buck.

Which is being gutted by two hunters; one is holding open its rear legs while the other crouches down and works with a knife. They wear winter-white camo jackets and have rifles slung over their backs—it's the same two guys she saw during the actual deer season.

"Stop! Get away!" Sarah shouts, and speeds forward.

"What?" her father calls from the bouncing sled behind.

She brakes at the kill site and hops off. "That's my deer!" she shouts. "What are you doing?"

The men stand up. Both have dark beards. The one doing the gutting has bloody, bare forearms and is holding a large knife in his right hand. Its blade glistens red.

"Your deer? We've been tracking this guy for days," the nearer one says.

"So what? I shot it," Sarah says. By now Art is standing beside her, with her mother on the other side.

"Shot it? With what?" the man with the knife says. "I don't see no gun."

"Me neither," the second man says. "Besides, y'all don't look much like hunters."

"I shot it with my .410," Sarah says.

Both men laugh at this. "A .410? This buck? Yeah, right, honey!"

"Listen, you—," Nat begins.

Art puts a hand on her shoulder and steps forward. "I'll take care of this."

"He'll take care of this," the taller hunter mimics.

"What she says is true," Art says. "She has a .410, this is her first deer, and you're stealing it from her."

The men are silent.

"Stealing from a girl," Art says.

"Kind of a cute one, too," the one with the knife says.

"That's for sure," the other hunter says. He swivels his rifle around so that its stock rests on his boots.

"Her mom ain't no dog either," the closer hunter says.

They both laugh hoarsely.

"Takes a real man to threaten a woman," Artie says, and steps forward.

"Dad—just let it go," Sarah breathes.

"That's a good plan," the hunter with the knife says. He points it at Artie. "Little man, why don't you just get back on your sled and leave."

Art sucks in a long, slow breath—tenses his body.

Suddenly the dark eye of the rifle muzzle is trained on

him. "Maybe you didn't hear me," the gunman says. "We don't want to have some kind of shooting accident."

"Yeah," the knife man says. "Out in the woods they happen all the time."

"Come on, Dad," Sarah murmurs urgently. "Let it go."

"How do you live with yourselves?" Artie says to them as Sarah pushes him back toward the snowmobile.

"This helps," the gunman says, and holds up his rifle.

"Have a good ride in the sled, Pops," the knife man says to Art. "Let your girls take you home now."

When they are out of sight of the poachers, Sarah lets the snowmobile coast to a stop. She leans forward onto the handlebars, and her shoulders begin to heave.

"Hey, it's all right," her mother says, and holds her tightly from behind.

"No, it's not all right," her father says.

Sarah looks back at him, then starts to cry again. "What are we going to tell Miles?"

Her parents are silent. Then her mother says, "We'll tell him that you wounded the deer."

Art gets out of the sled and puts a hand on her shoulder.

"That you thought it was dead, but it must not have

been," Nat adds. "It—I don't know—just got away."

"I wanted to show him," Sarah blubbers. "Prove to him that I could do it. That we can *do* this."

"We are doing it," Nat says.

"Sort of," Artie says. He is standing tree straight and looking back down the trail.

"Why would they take my deer?" Sarah asks, turning to her father. Her voice sounds like a weepy little girl, which only makes things worse.

"Because they could," he says. There is an edge, a harshness in his voice that she has never heard before.

CHAPTER TWENTY-EIGHT

MILES

THE WOUNDED DEER GOT AWAY. Sarah and his mother are totally upset, but his father is weirdly calm. He even wants to shoot Miles's big twelve gauge, so Miles shows him the safety button on it, then sends him outside. He would go with his father, but the sunlight is too bright today, and then there's the loud-noise thing.

Ka-poom! goes the long gun near the cabin.

"There goes the neighborhood," Miles says as he burrows back into his sleeping bag.

Sarah does not reply. She's totally buried in her bag.

"Sorry about your deer," Miles says. "With hunting,

that happens sometimes."

"It's not the deer," she says, her voice muffled.

"I don't get it then," Miles says.

"Leave me alone," she says.

"Okay," Miles says at length.

As the next few days pass, there's a different vibe in the cabin. His parents argue a lot, though they keep their voices low enough that he can't really hear what's going on. Ray is around, which means it's a weekend. He and Sarah usually disappear into the spear house, but today they are hanging around the cabin.

"Mom? Ray and I are going to use the sauna, okay?"

"The sauna?" Nat says. Art is outside somewhere, and Miles is relaxing by carving a piece of soft pine into the shape of a sunfish: a new fishing decoy. Nat glances at Miles, then at Ray and Sarah. "Okay. I guess. Is it warm in there?"

"Should be toasty by now," Sarah says. "We started a fire in the stove a half hour ago."

Nat pauses to stare at Ray and Sarah, who are holding hands. "I presume you'll be wearing your bathing suits or something?"

"Mother! Of course!" Sarah screeches, and pulls

Ray outside after her.

"Sweet," Miles says, and has a laugh—the first one in a while—then squints, waiting for the stabbing headache pain. But nothing. And none so far today.

"Really," Nat grumbles. "Sometimes I wonder about those two."

"Sarah's a big girl," Miles says.

"That's why I worry," his mother replies.

Poom! goes the shotgun outside.

Miles flinches, then glances toward the window. "What's with him? He's always packing these days."

Nat looks at the frosty glass as well. "You know what they say about people who carry guns?"

"No, what?"

"The more people who carry guns, the fewer people who carry guns."

Miles pauses for a moment. "I get it. But don't worry, he's careful."

"We were never a gun family. And look at us now." His mother is close to getting all weepy.

"Hey, things change," Miles says.

"I just worry about . . . ," she says, and sniffles briefly.

"I hope you don't worry about me," Miles says.

His mother looks at him; her eyes momentarily brim

up. "You're my number-one worry."

"My headaches are way better. They're not all the way gone, but they're a lot less than a month ago."

Big mistake, because his mother comes over and wraps him up in a big hug. "You do look better lately. You don't have that crazy stare."

"Thanks," Miles says sarcastically.

"I mean, not crazy crazy," his mother fumbles.

It's a good moment—interrupted by boots on the porch. It's Artie, carrying a partridge.

"Whoa!" Miles says.

"Did you shoot that?" Nat says.

"No," Art replies, leaning the gun against the wall and shucking off his parka. "It flew into a tree and broke its neck—right in front of me. Grouse suicide."

"Way to go, Dad!" Miles says.

"Miles says he's feeling better today," Nat says.

"That's good," Art says. "Maybe he'll be up for a trip one of these days."

"Trip? Like to town?" Miles asks.

"Farther," Art says with a glance to Nat.

She swallows and gets a seriously worried look.

"Where?" Miles asks. "Tell me what's going on!"

His father comes over, sits down by Miles, and holds

his hands close to the woodstove. "When you're up for it, we're going back to Birch Bay."

"Birch Bay!" Miles exclaims.

His father nods. "We're going to take back our cabin."

"And the squatters?" Miles asks. "What if they're still there?"

"I've got a plan," Artic says. "And living near Brainerd will put us within striking distance of Minneapolis—it's only a hundred and thirty miles—so you can get the medical care you need. From there we'll figure out the rest of our lives." He says this as if all of it is no big deal.

"Seriously, what if big Danny and the others are still in our cabin?" Miles asks.

His father shrugs. "We drive them off. Like they did us."

Miles stares at his father. His hair is longer and grayer; but his cheeks are red from the fresh, cold air, and in his wool cap he looks like a true outdoorsman. A tough guy.

"Cool," Miles says. "I'm in."

CHAPTER TWENTY-NINE

SARAH

"I'M REALLY SORRY ABOUT MY mom," Sarah says. She and Ray are in the sauna, lying on benches across from each other, a candle on the floor in between. Its little flame flickers from a small, chilly draft under the floor; but the wooden enclosure is 110 degrees, and the temperature is climbing.

"I thought it was funny," Ray says.

He's wearing a towel. Only. Sarah has on her two-piece swimming suit, which feels as if it has shrunk, especially the top. She hunches her shoulders together self-consciously as she lies on her stomach.

"So do you, like, pour water on the stove?" Ray asks.

"If we want steam."

"Go for it," Ray says.

She turns over on her side and scoops up a double handful of snow from a pail—throws it on the barrel stove. There's a sharp hiss, and the snow explodes into steam.

"Wow!" Ray says, then squints and leans away from the sudden cloud of hot, moist air.

Sarah laughs. "You asked for it."

"That almost burned my lungs," Ray says, breathing with his mouth open.

"It's not that hot," she says.

He hangs on to his towel as he turns over onto his side so he can see her.

"But hot is good," he says, letting his eyes travel over her.

She lets her eyes travel down his flat belly—then looks away. The burning wood in the stove snaps and pops.

"I wish I had my sketch pad," he says.

"Why? The pages would probably catch on fire."

"Which reminds me of that old joke," Ray says. "Is it hot in here—"

"—or is it just me?" Sarah finishes. She giggles.

"It's you," Ray says. "And anyway, I don't really need my pad 'cause I'll remember you like this." He holds up his hands as if to look at her through a picture frame. "Exactly as you are right now."

She swallows. "My parents are talking about leaving here," she blurts. "To be closer to Minneapolis."

"I know," Ray answers. He lies back and stares at the wood above him.

"You do?!"

"My dad told me they were discussing it."

"It's more than 'discussing' with my dad. He's totally fixated on taking back our cabin in Brainerd."

Ray is silent. Then he says, "So what would happen to us?" It just falls out of his mouth unself-consciously—which is what she has always liked about him.

"It's not like we're engaged," she says. It's supposed to be a joke—one of those quick comebacks that guarantee a laugh.

A shadow passes over Ray's face. He looks away.

"I'm sorry, Ray," she says.

"No, it's true," he says at length. "We're only fourteen."

"Ah, thirteen?"

He smiles. "You look fourteen. Actually, you look sixteen."

"Shut up," she says. "I do not!"

He turns his face sideways. "Yes, you do. Remember how Mackenzie was all about how old you were that first day?"

Sarah nods.

"That's because she's almost fifteen, I think."

"So she can be good in sports," Sarah says.

"Exactly. It used to be just boys who got held back a grade. Now girls do, too."

"I remember something else, too," Sarah says. "How the other girls said you drew them."

Ray nods.

"So how come you've never drawn me?"

"You don't need to be drawn. You're perfect as is."

"Yeah, right," she says, and looks away.

"But now, if you're leaving, maybe I should," Ray adds.

Sarah swallows.

"So I can really, really remember you," Ray says. He holds up his hands again in a small frame and looks through them.

"Like this?" She flips her hair over a shoulder, then arches her back and looks sideways at him like a movie star. She giggles.

"Like that," Ray says. There's something suddenly hoarse and choky in his voice.

She laughs and collapses back onto her belly. "Anyway, you'll have your driver's license in two years. If we're living in Brainerd, that's only two hours from here. You can drive down and see me."

"Two years? Forget that," Rays says. "With luck I'll get into the arts school in Minneapolis next year for ninth grade. Then I can see you all the time."

"Arts school—that's where they have naked models, right?" Sarah teases.

"'Life' models," Ray says. "That's what they're called."

Sarah giggles. "I know that. But they're still naked."

CHAPTER THIRTY

MILES

WINTER BREAKS WEIRDLY EARLY, at the end of February. The news is all about the clearing skies and return to "travel as normal"; though the restricted-movement law is still in place, no one is enforcing it. Which is good, because they are leaving for Birch Bay.

The first stop is at Ray's house to borrow the O'Keefes' van for the trip south.

"Are you sure you can get by without your car for a while?" Nat asks them.

"For sure," Herb says.

"It's good practice in being car free," Mrs. O'Keefe

adds. She's a tall, slightly wild-haired woman who smells of patchouli oil; she has the same dark eyes and liveliness as Ray.

Ray and Sarah are standing glued together like branches from the same tree. She has been all weepy lately, as if it's finally dawning on her that she won't be seeing Ray every day of her life.

"But what about Mr. Kurz's cabin?" Sarah says, as if that would change things.

"It's not going anywhere," Miles says.

"I'll check on it once in a while," Herb says. "Maybe even try some fishing."

"And if it doesn't work out at Birch Bay, we'll come back," Nat says.

"It will work out," Artie says.

They all look at him.

"But how will we get their van back?" Sarah asks; it's as if she's grasping at straws, trying to find some way to stay closer to Ray.

"Herb and I have that figured out," Artie says. "Don't worry about it."

"What about your snowmobile?" Sarah says to Miles.

"Back to Old But Gold," Miles says.

There is silence; Sarah has run out of reasons to stay.

"You'll be careful, right?" Herb says to Artie as they shake hands. "No crazy stuff?"

"No crazy stuff," Artie says.

Sarah leans her head on Ray's shoulder. He looks as if he might cry, too.

"That's enough, you two," Nat says. It's supposed to be a joke, but Sarah pooches out her lower lip as if she is nine years old.

"Are you sure Sarah wouldn't like to stay here?" Mrs. O'Keefe says. "We'd be happy to look after her."

"I don't think so," Nat says immediately, with a glance at Ray. "It's a family thing," she adds in a softer tone. "We need to be together."

And, minutes later, they are rolling out of Bemidji as Sarah sobs in the rear seat.

Miles rolls his eyes. His mother puts a finger to her lips. "Just let her vent," she whispers.

"Puppy love," Miles says.

"Shut up, Miles!" Sarah says.

Artie drives. Not fast so as to attract attention, but not slowly either. Miles rides shotgun—literally. The twelve gauge, loaded, rests loosely across his lap, and the traffic is very light and free-flowing. He glances at his father, who sits ramrod straight in the seat, with both hands on the wheel. He keeps his eyeballs moving—checking the mirrors, the sides of the road, behind them—on full alert. Miles allows himself to lean back in the seat and let his own eyelids slip shut. His father is a different guy than the last time they arrived at Birch Bay. . . .

Soon, through the trees, we saw the brown roofline. Then the glint of window glass and the coppery log front of the cabin. But in the yard everything was changed. We drew up to stare.

A car, a late-model sedan, sat parked on the side and covered with ash.

Other stuff that he can't pull back. But he lets it go, moves on with his dream, fragmented bits of his memory.

Another older car, without wheels, sat halfway into the trees. A large, shiny Harley perched on the porch . . . wooden steps, which looked chewed and splintered.

. . . Behind the house came the chak *sound of an axe splitting wood. Some kind of animal went "baa!" . . . Only the lake was the same. Gull Lake sparkled—as always—in the sunlight.*

"What the hell is going on here!" my mother yelled. She stalked forward.

"Wait. Nat! Go carefully!" my father said.

But that only made my mother pick up her pace. . . . After all, it was our cabin.

The house smelled of cooking, garlic. . . . A couple of small children were playing cars and dolls on the stone floor . . . normal-looking little kids in summer clothes . . . rushed away . . calling, "Momma! Daddy!"

. . . shirtless, pale and out of shape . . . "What are you doing in our house?" Sarah said.

The man swallowed and looked behind him. A woman holding a baby appeared. . . . ordinary mother.

"Your house?" the woman said. Something caught in her voice.

"That's right," my mother said. "I'm Natalie Newell, this is my family, and you're in our cabin."

"Listen," the man began, stammering slightly. "I'm Rick and this is my wife, Ruth. . . ."

"We could care less who you are," Sarah said, her voice getting hysterical. "Get out!"

The man's wife, Ruth, did not smile. ". . . knew this would happen."

"We've been here for nearly a year," he said, as if that was supposed to explain everything.

"And now it's time for you and your family to leave," my mother said. . . .

"Things are different now. . . ."

"Yes, that's right, different," his wife murmured.

"Hey—what the hell's going on?" a louder voice boomed . . .

large man . . . wore a black T-shirt that covered his big chest but not his round belly . . . bandana held back long stringy hair. His full beard was peppered with sawdust, and he held an axe.

Alongside him appeared another woman who was dressed like him—they looked like a biker couple . . . wood chips on her black, sleeveless T-shirt.

"So the absentee owners finally appear," the man said with a grin.

. . . All of us looked at each other; nobody spoke. By now the children, including two more for a total of five, peeked out from behind the adults.

". . . get the sheriff," my mother said. She looked to my father.

The dream comes into sharper focus now. Like a jerky movie playing in his head.

The woman holding the baby spoke up. "The sheriff is my brother. . . ."

My mother stared.

". . . said it was all right for us to stay here. We're from Chicago, and we couldn't stay there, not in the city, not with the children, so we came here," she continued in a rush. "You don't know how bad things were—"

"That's enough," her husband said.

"Things is different nowadays," Danny added. "The rules have changed."

"*And who are you?*" *my mother asked, turning to the biker.*

"*Me and Sheila, we're the real squatters,*" *big Danny said. He had teeth missing on top.* "*We were here first, and then Rick and Ruth came along with their three kids and we took them in.*"

"*You took them in?*" *my mother said, her voice rising.*

"*That's right,*" *the big man said easily.* "*A nice big place like this, just sitting empty—hell, there was room for two families.*"

My mother narrowed her eyes in her I'm-counting-to-ten mode.

"*I'll tell you what,*" *she said to the people in our cabin.* "*I don't care if the sheriff is your uncle, your brother, or the Pope. I suggest you start packing.*"

. . . "*Daddy do we have to leave again?*" *one of the children whimpered.*

"*Shhh!*" *Ruth said.*

. . . "*Tell you what,*" *my father said.* . . . "*There's no rush here—as long as we all understand what needs to be done.*"

. . . *We walked down the steps . . . and back up the driveway. It was like we were zombies. Sarah blurted.* "*They just can't take our cabin. People can't do that!*"

. . . "*Let's give them some time,*" *my father said.*

Miles jerks awake—grabs for his gun.

"All good," his father says quickly as the van rolls along. He pats Miles on the arm.

They pass the campground where they stayed the night after the squatters drove them off, then in another half hour they arrive in Walker. The Dairy Queen is still closed for the winter. He tracks it with his eyes as they pass.

"Too bad!" Sarah says to Miles. "You were hoping that girl would be working."

"What girl?" Miles asks.

"The one who flirted with you when we stopped for ice cream," Sarah says. She's slumped in her seat but at least is paying attention to where they are.

"Girl?" Miles scratches his head in fake puzzlement. Art and Nat look at him with concern.

"The one with big brown eyes who was, like, way out of your league," Sarah adds.

"Oh, that one," Miles says.

Then it's south through the pine forest and lake country on Highway 371, and after forty minutes Artie signals and turns into a motel parking lot. It's a local, indie type of motel with a 1950s front and a few older "cabinettes" behind. Each numbered door has a dusty truck or car parked up close; at least half have flat tires, and some have curtains over the windows or newspaper taped to the glass.

"Where are we?" Sarah asks quickly; she has been dozing again.

"The Bradford Inn," Nat says. "I called ahead just to make sure we have a place to stay tonight. You know, in case . . ."

"I'll be right back," Artie says with a nod to Miles to stay with the van.

As they wait, they look at the shabby motel.

"The Bradford Inn," Miles says in a fake radio announcer's voice, "your best choice for a fun-filled family vacation."

"Right," Sarah says.

Artie comes out of the office. "We're set," he says. "At the Bradford Inn, cash is king."

"So we have a room reserved?" Sarah asks.

"Actually, a little cabinette," Artie says, nodding to the rear.

"They look smaller than Mr. Kurz's place," Sarah says.

"But they do have running water," Nat says. "Right?"

Artie nods as he accelerates down the highway. "But don't get your hopes up for staying at the Bradford.

Tonight we'll be back in our own place."

Miles shoots a sidelong glance at his mother, who looks scared.

In another twenty minutes they turn off the highway and start to wind along Gull Lake, which is mostly hidden through the trees. Every driveway has a gate or a chain across it, along with at least one NO TRESPASSING! or POSTED—KEEP OUT sign. Miles's stomach tightens— and so does his grip on the shotgun—as they near the narrow, curving driveway to Birch Bay.

Artie glances in the rearview mirror, then slows to a stop on the road by the old mailbox they know so well.

A chain lies limp across the driveway. In thin snow, a single dark motorcycle track crosses the downed chain.

"Damn," Artie breathes.

"They're still here," Miles says.

Sarah swallows. "Now what?" she asks.

"Let's just turn around and go," Nat says.

"But Danny's not around—at least not at the moment," Miles says.

"How do you know?" Nat asks.

"The chain is down, and there's his track," Miles replies; he glances behind, down the narrow road.

"Which means he's coming back," Nat says.

"Exactly," Art and Miles say at the same time.

"The chain!" Art says to Miles—who throws him a thumbs-up sign.

"I'm there," Miles says.

It takes them only minutes to get ready, to set their trap. Danny has had the chain strung between two oak trees, one on either side of the road, but two small trees—one pine, one aspen—are perfect: They are small enough to give, to bend, plus they are closer to the driveway entrance. Danny will be slowing but still rolling along nicely. With that the chain will suddenly be pulled tight and motorcycle high.

"I don't know about this," Nat says. "You don't want to kill him."

"It's not going to kill him," Miles says.

"I think it's brilliant," Sarah says.

"Guess you're outvoted," Miles says to his mother.

"So what do I do?" Nat asks.

"And me?" Sarah adds.

"You two are backups," Artie says. "If Miles and I screw up and he sees us, your job is to get us out of here."

"Shoot a couple of rounds in the air, then come driving up fast," Miles says.

"We can do that," Sarah says, glancing at her mom.

Nat swallows. "I just don't want you getting hurt!" she breathes. She's white-faced.

"Not to worry," Miles says.

"We'll have the side door of the van open," Sarah adds. "In case you have to dive in."

"Now you're talking," Miles says.

"Okay, tell me where to park," Nat says, sliding behind the wheel.

"Up ahead just around the corner. Be turned around so you're ready to roll," Miles says.

"Don't worry, we'll be ready," Sarah says as she lifts her shotgun.

They wait less than an hour for the rumble of a Harley. Artie signals to Miles, who ducks lower behind a tree trunk. He and his father crouch out of sight and have the chain ready to jerk Danny's bike.

Miles's heartbeat is thrash-punk fast by the time Danny comes into view on his long-forked bike. He gears down once, then again as he nears the driveway entrance. Swiveling his head, he looks suspiciously at the van parked up the road at the same time as he turns into the driveway.

Artie and Miles yank the chain upward and give each end a quick loop around a small tree. The chain spans the driveway chest high. Danny is looking to the side and never sees the chain, which clangs on his bike handlebars, then catches him in the chest and strips him off the Harley like an invisible hand swatting a fly.

Thoomp! goes Danny on his back onto the frozen ground; his bike rolls on crazily into some brush, where it tips over, roars briefly, then dies.

Miles and Artie hurry forward. Miles holds his shotgun on Danny just in case, but the biker lies on the ground gasping for air.

"Are you alive?" Artie asks as he crouches over him.

Danny makes noises and lifts his arms one at a time to make sure they work. "Not sure." He groans.

"Too bad," Artie says.

Danny blinks and blinks as if he can't place his attackers.

"The Newells?" Art says. "We live here, remember?"

Miles puts the muzzle of his shotgun in Danny's face; the biker's eyes go crossed as the steel eye closes in on his forehead.

"Don't shoot me!" Danny groans. "I'm injured. I

think I broke some ribs."

"It might be better to put you out of your misery," Artie says. He looks at Miles, who shrugs as if that would be simpler.

"Please," Danny says. "We'll pack up! We was thinking about leaving soon anyway."

At that moment the van with Nat and Sarah comes up fast and skids to a stop.

"The rest of the Newell family," Art says as Sarah and Nat hurriedly get out.

Sarah stands over Danny. "You remember me, don't you?" she asks.

He looks at her blankly.

"Well, I remember you!" She kicks his leg.

"Oww!" Danny says.

"Sarah, what's wrong with you!" Nat calls, and pulls her backward.

"My sister, Sarah," Miles says to Danny with a shrug. "You don't mess with her these days."

"I need to sit up." Danny groans.

They drag him upright and over to a tree; legs outstretched, he slumps back against the trunk. His narrow, snake-like eyes fall on Miles's shotgun.

"That ain't the gun I gave you," he says.

"I needed something with more stopping power," Miles says.

Danny's gaze flickers back and forth between the Newells. "You was just a bunch of city folks the last time I saw you. Now you're all gunned up. What do you think you're gonna do, shoot me?" he says to Miles. A hint of scorn creeps back into his voice.

"We don't necessarily need guns," Artie says. He produces his shiny trimming axe, turns to face a tree, and throws it end over end. *Thunk!*—the axehead buries itself in the wood.

Danny's eyes widen.

"So here's the deal," Artie says as he retrieves his axe. "We're going to go down to the cabin and have a talk. Your job is to tell everyone that you're all leaving— today."

"We got nowhere to go!" Danny says. He is not so injured that he doesn't try for sympathy.

"Yes, you do," Artie says, stepping forward.

Danny looks suspiciously at him.

"Do you know the Bradford Inn up on Highway 371?"

"Yeah," Danny says sullenly.

"That's where you're going. There's a cabinette

waiting for you," Artie says. "It's reserved in our name, but you can have it."

"I ain't got money to rent no cabin," Danny says.

"We've already paid for two weeks. That'll give you time to figure out your next move."

Danny narrows his eyes. "Why would you do that?"

"Because we're not you," Sarah answers.

CHAPTER THIRTY-ONE

SARAH

THEIR TAKEOVER OF BIRCH BAY is not complete until big Danny and his wife, Sheila (the woman who gave Emily to Sarah), and their two kids have loaded their stuff into the rear of the van.

"Well, I guess we all survived the winter," Sheila ventures as she pushes in one last duffel bag.

"As if that makes things all right?" Nat says to Sheila; Nat is slowly getting her edge back.

"What happened to that family who you took in?" Artie asks. "They had little kids."

"I don't know," Sheila says with a dark glance to

Danny. "One morning we got up and they were gone."

Danny shrugs, then winces and holds his ribs.

"And Emily the goat—how'd she work out?" Sheila asks Sarah.

Sarah swallows. "Fine."

"Okay, let's go," Artie says quickly to Danny and Sheila. He steers Danny to the passenger seat, where he settles in with a groan.

"Be careful, Dad!" Sarah calls to Artie.

"Don't worry," Sheila says, "he's not going to cause any more trouble—are you, Danny?"

Danny lowers his chin like a beaten man.

"And anyway, we got your Harley," Miles says.

"We'll come back for the bike when he's in riding shape," Sheila says as she buckles Danny's seat belt.

Danny winces. "Be careful!"

"Buck up," Sheila says. "You had a worse wreck down in Sturgis that time."

And with that the van pulls away.

"We're way too nice to those people," Sarah says.

Back inside the cabin, they survey the damage. There are ashtrays full of cigarette butts everywhere, but the loon art is still on the wall, and the piece of driftwood she found when she was five—the one that looks like an exploding star—is still on the fireplace mantel. The place is messy and stinky but not wrecked. Not like Mr. Kurz's place when they first arrived.

"Well, I guess it's cabin-cleaning time," Nat says.

"Again," Sarah says with fake sarcasm.

"Hey, the electricity is even on!" Miles says. He flicks a light switch on and off; the wagon wheel light fixture flashes brightly.

"I wonder who paid the power bill," Nat says.

"Probably Danny's wife," Art says.

"My cell phone charger is in the van!" Sarah says.

"Another hour without it won't hurt you," Miles says.

"Shut up, Miles," Sarah replies.

"Children!" Nat says. "I hope we're not falling back into our same old patterns."

"You mean like everybody taking a long shower every day, and using up lots of electricity?" Miles says as Nat heads toward the bathroom.

"Hot water and soap are not a bad thing," she calls back.

"Yeah, Miles!" Sarah says.

But he has turned to look at himself in the mirror. It's an antique, with slightly smoky glass and a frame of birchbark; he leans closer and squints at himself.

"What?" Sarah asks.

"I . . . could use a haircut." It's as if he was going to say more but doesn't.

"Well, I could use a total makeover," Sarah says. She pulls off her wool sweater, then sniffs it.

"You've already had one," Miles says, glancing at her in the mirror, then again at himself from another angle.

"Gee, thanks, bro," she says.

But Miles doesn't reply. He keeps staring at his face in the mirror.

The next week goes fast and slow. It takes two days of washing the walls with vinegar and water to get rid of the cigarette smell. Another full day on the window glass and log furniture; some of the cushions have so many cigarette burns and wine stains that they have to be thrown away.

Artie does the bathroom, Nat the kitchen.

"Pigs," Nat says, her voice muffled by a bandana over her mouth; she is on her hands and knees scrubbing the floor; the soapy water in the pail is dark brown.

"We're getting there," Sarah calls. For the first time in her life she doesn't mind cleaning; her towel squeaks across the clean window glass. Beyond are leafless trees and the dull gray ice of Gull Lake—but dead-looking ice is a good thing: Spring is coming.

By Wednesday (it feels strange to look at a calendar again) the lake ice honeycombs and starts to melt; by Friday big sheets of it break apart and grind against one another from a warm southern breeze. It's her favorite sound, one she remembers as a kid—that tinkling, crushing, grinding sound when the ice begins to move.

On Saturday Sarah waits anxiously for Ray and his dad to come and retrieve their van. Artie and Nat have bought a used vehicle in Brainerd, a generic minivan not unlike the O'Keefes'—the kind she would not have been caught dead in back in the suburbs—so now they at least have wheels. They offered to drive the O'Keefes' van back north, but Ray saw a Craigslist ride to Brainerd.

And anyway, I want to see Birch Bay, he texted.

Sarah and her father drive to Brainerd and wait at a gas station, where they are planning to meet Ray and his dad.

Ten more miles!!!! Ray texts. Sarah's stomach does its own little ice-out dance, but she tries to stay cool.

Artie glances up at the gas station signs. "Ten bucks a gallon. I hope it stays that way," he remarks.

"Why?" Sarah asks. She squints down the highway.

There are only a few cars, and soon one of them has to be Ray's.

"People will drive less, and our country can stop getting into wars over oil."

"Uh-huh," Sarah says distractedly.

N I have a present for U2, Ray texts.

"Maybe the volcanoes will finally make us go green," her father says, but she hardly hears him because an older car pulls in, with Ray's smiling face in the side window.

"That's them," Artie says.

"Where?" Sarah says as if she hasn't noticed.

Herb and Artie shake hands. Sarah and Ray give each other a brief, totally casual hug, then stand around looking at their fathers. Ray is holding his ever-present sketch pad.

"Thanks again for coming down," Artie says. "Let's head over to Birch Bay and get you your van back!"

"We got along just fine without it," Herb says.

In the rear seat, Sarah and Ray hold hands. "Drawing stuff on the way down?" Sarah giggles.

"Nope. But I've been drawing a lot lately. My best stuff," he says; his eyes shine.

"Show me," Sarah says.

"Not here," Ray mouths.

They make small talk on the ten-minute ride, and soon the cabin is in sight.

Ray looks out the window. "Just like I imagined it," he said. "Kind of old-school."

"Belonged to my father," Artie says.

Inside the cabin, a birch log fire crackles, and there's the smell of fresh cookies.

"Miles! How are you doing?" Herb asks immediately, and comes over to shake his hand.

"I'm sorry—do I know you?"

Herb pauses, then laughs.

Miles doesn't. Sarah glances at him. Sometimes it's hard to tell when Miles is joking, which is the worrisome part.

"My neuro-shrink says I'm ninety percent there," Miles says. He shrugs as if he doesn't quite agree.

"With you, ninety percent is plenty," Nat says.

"I'd say so, too," Artie says.

As the adults talk, Sarah nods her head to Ray, and they slide away down the hall, toward the kids' bedrooms.

"So let's see," she says, her gaze on his sketch pad.

He swallows as if he's suddenly shy. "I hope you'll be all right with this," he says, and opens the wide pages.

She sucks in her breath. "It's me. In the sauna!"

Ray is silent. She turns to him; his face is both excited and apprehensive—as if she might be angry with him.

Her eyes go back to the page. "It's really good," she says. "But was my back that sweaty?"

He laughs. "Yes, for sure." He puts his arm around her as they look at the drawing.

It's only black-and-gray pencil lines on heavy white paper, with some shadow areas rubbed in, but it's totally real. And totally sexy.

"Did I really look that good?" she asks with a quick glance over her shoulder toward the doorway.

"Better," Ray says.

They have time for one kiss before the adult voices in the living room change in tone, as if people might be getting up and moving around.

"Anyway, the drawing is for you," Ray says.

She pauses. Looks at it again. "Um, my mom and dad might freak if they saw it."

"It's not like you're naked," Ray says, "though I could erase a couple of lines and you would be."

"You better not!" Sarah says with a giggle. She glances again over her shoulder. "I have a better idea! You should use it as part of your art school application."

"And anyway, we have two spare bedrooms—," Nat

says overly loudly as the adults come down the hall. She's showing Herb around.

Sarah claps shut the sketch pad, and she and Ray manage to be standing by the window, with Sarah pretending to point at something of interest across the lake.

"Nice," Herb says, and they move on.

"Don't be antisocial, kids," Nat says over her shoulder to Sarah.

Back in the living room they all have coffee and cookies.

"So, what's next for you all?" Herb asks.

"This will work for the time being," Artie says, glancing around at the cabin.

"No major moves until Miles is ready," Nat says more firmly.

Miles rolls his eyes with annoyance.

"But what about your other house in Wayzata?" Ray asks.

Silence falls across the living room.

"Another cookie?" Nat asks, and hands Ray the plate.

At the end of May, when Miles is at his appointment at the hospital in Minneapolis with Nat, Sarah and Artie slip away and drive west across the city.

"You didn't have to come," Artie says as he drives.

Sarah swallows. "I wanted to."

Neither of them says much after that.

Entering the suburbs, they pass streets where every third house has plywood over its windows and doors. The houses that remain occupied have metal grates over the windows; they are made to look decorative, but they are still bars—the kind that used to be found only in the toughest neighborhoods of Minneapolis. Lawn signs announce home security systems. One McMansion with a long driveway has a sign reading TRESPASSERS WILL BE SHOT hung on a crudely installed gate.

"Not good," Artie murmurs as they turn into the last street before their cul-de-sac.

"Hey, there's Dr. Carapezzi," Sarah says.

Artie slows.

Dr. Carapezzi, a retired dentist who never minded Sarah and Miles biking endlessly up and down the street and goofing around the cul-de-sac, has come outside to check his mailbox. Wearing a long, heavy bathrobe, he has his hand on the mailbox door just as Artie slows the van.

Sarah powers down her window and leans out. "Hello!"

Dr. Carapezzi whirls and steps back. One hand goes into his robe pocket, which hangs heavy.

"Dr. Carapezzi. It's me. Sarah Newell? From up the cul-de-sac?"

The man squints for long moments.

"My brother and I used to ride our bikes all the time around here."

He blinks, then walks quickly away, making sure to look over his shoulder a couple of times—and always keeping his hand in his pocket—before he disappears into his house.

Artie shrugs, then drives on. She holds her breath as their big house comes into view.

"Well, it's still here!" Artie says.

"No Harleys out front," Sarah adds.

As Artie pulls up the driveway, Sarah's eyes go to the broken windows. The front door that hangs askew.

"Not good," Artie mutters, and lets out a long breath.

They get out. There is silence all around.

They listen again, then slowly approach the house. With his foot, Artie pushes open the door. It squeaks, then clangs.

The smell hits her—a horrible stench worse than any outhouse or dead animal.

"My God!" Artie says, and squints from the smell.

They step forward into the foyer, which is far enough to see the damage. The furniture is smashed or cut. White stuffing boils out of the leather couches and armchairs. Someone has had a fire in the fireplace. Charred pieces of chair frames—arms and legs—lie cold and half burned.

"I never liked those dining-room chairs," Artie says.

But Sarah can't speak, because she can barely catch her breath. The kitchen is gutted: Sheetrock caved in and copper pipes stripped. All the copper kettles—the designer set—are missing. The refrigerator is tipped over, and black mold beards the open door.

And the stink worsens—makes her eyes water—and she covers her nose with her forearm as they move down the hallway.

"Wait here," Artie says to her—and she's happy to obey.

Soon she hears her father gag; then he comes quickly back and waves her toward the front door.

"What?" Sarah asks.

"The bathrooms," Artie says. He gags once more but keeps it together without puking. "The pipes must have frozen and the toilets were turned off—but whoever was here just kept using them."

Near the van he slugs down a half bottle of water as Sarah stares at their house. Their wrecked house.

"So what do we do now?" she whispers.

After a pause her father says, "I don't think anyone can live in it again. Once the city inspectors get to this neighborhood, our house will probably be condemned."

"Meaning?" Though really, she knows.

"Meaning it's a public health hazard. It will be torn down," her father says. Weirdly, there is little emotion in his voice.

"Mom," Sarah begins, then chokes up. "What about Mom?"

Artie puts an arm around Sarah. "She loved this place. It was her dream house."

Sarah nods.

"But you know what?" her father says. "I never did. It always felt . . . empty to me. No matter how much stuff we put in it."

They are silent again. Artie turns to the garage, and Sarah follows. The door is smashed in. Miles's tools are scattered around as if the vandals were looking for something more valuable. As if his wrenches and sockets and clamps and pliers were useless.

Back outside they take one last look at the house.

"Do we just . . . leave it here?" Sarah asks. "Walk away?"

"There should be some insurance money," Art says. "Unless the insurance company tries to screw us with some 'act of God' thing. About the volcanoes, I mean."

"And what if they do?" Sarah asks. "Will we be all right?"

"Are we all right now?" he says.

She pauses, then nods.

"Okay then," he says with a little smile, and gives her a quick hug. He checks his watch. "We'd better get back to the hospital."

On the way, her father detours through south Minneapolis. The neighborhood where they lived before they moved to the suburbs. People are out on streets, and watchful, but none seem to be packing. He slows past the Newell family's first house, a narrow two-story that needs painting. It has window grates, but a family is sitting on the front porch. A couple of young mini-gangstas hang out at the corner.

"Mom always worried about this neighborhood," Sarah says, "but I never did."

"Me neither," her father says.

They arrive back at the hospital just in time: Miles and Nat are coming down the stairs. Nat is smiling.

"The doc says I may yet have a career playing high-stakes poker," Miles calls to them.

"Great!" Sarah says with major sarcasm.

"What have you two been up to?" Nat says. She lifts one dark eyebrow; she has great radar.

Sarah glances at her father, who is silent.

"Nothing," Sarah says quickly.

"Well, not truly nothing," Artie says.

Miles and Nat wait; it's as if they know.

"We took a little drive," Artie begins.

"And?" Miles says quickly.

"We went . . ." He pauses. It's as if he doesn't want to say 'home.' "Sarah and I went back to our old house."

Nat swallows. "And?"

"It's still there," Artie begins.

"Thank God!" Nat says.

"But not really," Sarah says quickly.

"We can't go back," Art explains. "It's wrecked."

Nat sucks in a breath. She has to sit down. "I sort of knew that in my bones," she says.

"What about my stuff? My tools?" Miles asks.

"Still pretty much all there," Sarah says. "It's like

nobody knew how to use them."

"Sweet," Miles says.

After a long moment Nat stands up. "All right then, let's go home," she says. "Wherever that may be."

"Home is where they understand you," Sarah replies with a glance toward Miles.

"Garfield," Miles says immediately. "Right after he kisses Odie."

"Say no more, bro," Sarah says. She takes Miles's arm and leads her family through the door.

MEMORY BOY

Did you miss *Memory Boy,* the first book about Miles and Sarah? Here's a peek at what happened before *The Survivors!*

NOW OR NEVER

IT WAS THE PERFECT TIME for leaving. Weather conditions were finally right: a steady breeze blew from the south, plus there was just enough moonlight to see by.

July 3, 2008.

This would be the date our family would always remember, assuming, of course, that we lived to tell about it.

"Hurry up. The wind won't last forever," I said. Three shadowy figures—my sister, Sarah, and my parents— fumbled with their luggage. With me, we were the Newell family. We lived in west suburban Minneapolis—for a few more minutes, at least.

"Shut up, Miles," Sarah muttered. She was twelve going on thirteen, and her carry-on bag overflowed with last-minute additions. I couldn't complain; I had my own private stuff, including a small sealed jar that would be hard to explain to my family. So I didn't try. Right now one of Sarah's stupid paperbacks dropped with a thud onto the sidewalk. I sighed and went to help her.

"I'm not leaving," Sarah said, jerking away from me. "Everybody's going to die anyway, so why can't we die in our own house?" She plopped down onto the lawn. Pale pumice puffed up around her and hung in the air like a ghostly double. That was the weird thing about the volcanic ash; it had been falling softly, softly falling, for over two years now—and sometimes it was almost beautiful. Tonight the rock flour suspended in the air made a wide, furry-white halo around the moon. Its giant, raccoon-like eyeball stared down and made the whole neighborhood look X-rayed.

"Nobody's going to die," I said. "Though if we stay in the city, we might," I muttered to myself.

"How do you know?" Sarah said. She sat there stubbornly, clutching her elbows.

"Actually, I don't. Which is why we're leaving."

Sarah swore at me. Anything logical really pissed her off these days.

"Arthur!" my mother said sharply to my father. "Help out anytime."

My father coughed briefly and stepped forward. "Think of it this way, Sarah. We're heading to the lake," he said, his voice muffled under his dust mask. "We'll get to our cabin, kick back, ride this out. Swiss Family Robinson all the way." He manufactured a short laugh that fell about fifty yards short of sincere. Sometimes I worried more about him than my sister and mother; they at least knew how to put wood in a fireplace. My father was a real city guy, a musician, a jazz drummer.

My mother added, "We all agreed, remember? As Miles said, up at Birch Bay we'll have more control of things, like heat, food, and water. When things improve—when the ash stops falling, and when there's gasoline, and when the food stores are full again—we'll come back home." Something, maybe the dust, caught briefly in her throat.